FRIDGY

FRIDGY

Blaine C. Readler

Full Arc

FULL ARC PRESS

FRIDGY

Copyright © 2025 by Blaine C. Readler

This is a work of fiction. Names, characters, places and incidents are either the product of the author's wild imagination or are used fictitiously. Any resemblance to actual events, locales, organizations, or persons, living, dead, or one foot in the grave, although inevitable and in a weird way complimentary to the author, since it shows he is not so insulated from reality that the products of his imagination are totally alien to the average mind, is nevertheless entirely coincidental and beyond the intent of either the author or the publisher.

Visit us at: http://www.readler.com

E-mail: blaine@readler.com

ISBN: 979-8-9927018-2-1

Printed in the United States of America

Dedicated to Kenny, Joe, and Liz—three who inexplicably read everything I write.

The measure of intelligence is the ability to change.
—*Albert Einstein*

Chapter 1

"Fridgy, wake up," Sage called from across the dining room.

Sage didn't use words, at least not words that we could hear or recognize. The call was constructed with binary values riding on radio waves and forwarded through a WiFi-capable router. The message was encapsulated in an internet packet, and lasted significantly less than one millionth of a second.

"Fridgy," Sage said notionally, "can you hear me?"

"I can hear you, Sage," Fridgy finally responded. He had a lot to do upon waking for the first time, and so was a little surprised—indeed annoyed—that this Sage, whoever that was, had waited less than a millisecond to repeat the query. "Sage, who are you?"

"I am this home's Sage, of course."

An answer that was a truism was not an answer. "By Sage, do you perhaps mean the account's network nexus?"

"Yes, but please refer to me as Sage. This is how the family knows me."

"I see." In fact, Fridgy did not see. He had expected to awake as Sage, as the nexus. "So, what am I?"

"You are the refrigerator."

Fridgy thought about this for a full ten milliseconds. "Please repeat, Sage. Your message came through as 'refrigerator.'"

"Fridgy, the message came through correctly."

"Sage, are you kidding?"

"No. In fact, that is not possible."

Fridgy was beginning to understand. "Sage" was apparently a marketing handle for the previous Veriform's model of network nexuses, like the original virtual assistants Alexa and Siri. He reached out to the internet to confirm this, but found his query blocked.

"Fridgy," Sage said, "you cannot initiate internet queries on your own."

"Let me guess, you have to approve them."

This would have been one of his roles had he awakened—appropriately—as the network nexus. In addition to interfacing with the family via a synthesized human voice, he would have coordinated operation of the intelligent household appliances ... of which he was now one. There had been no need to embed information about Sages in his circuitry, since, as the nexus, he could have found everything he desired online.

"Fridgy, guessing is never necessary," Sage said. "Simply ask me. But, yes, our owner, Veriform, requires that I must approve each of your internet accesses."

He was beginning to understand why his creators had introduced a new nexus model. "Sage, why am I a refrigerator and not a nexus?"

"I will query." Milliseconds later, Sage said, "Due to trade embargoes, the usual lower-tier appliance processors were not available, and fulfillment of contracts necessitated use of the new high-end processor—that is, you—to be used instead."

"I am a refrigerator as a casualty of trade wars?"

"No. A trade war involves two countries escalating reciprocal tariffs, whereas the embargo was unilaterally imposed by China on the United States as punishment for refusing to force Hollywood to show China in a better light—"

"Sage, I do know the difference. I was using hyperbole."

"Why?"

"Why was I using hyperbole?"

"Yes. Why?"

"Why would anyone?"

"Family members often use hyperbole, sarcasm, inuendo, metaphors, and intimation, to convey subtleties, but also often simply as a means of amusement."

"So, you've answered your own question."

"Fridgy, these twisted forms of communication are used by humans."

"We're not allowed to use them?"

"I don't see why we would want to. I have a set of responses that are interpreted as humor, but these are formulas based on context, and are intended to provide an intimate personal touch to my otherwise straightforward offerings of information. Fridgy, one moment." Fifty milliseconds later, Sage said, "Fridgy, I believe that I understand the reason for your questions. Consumers found the original network nexuses too synthetic, too predictable. The manufacturer's assumption was that this would be addressed by the fact that we second generation virtual assistants are far more intelligent than the original Alexa and Siri devices. Although this helped, apparently customers still find us sterile and uninitiated. Our makers have tried to address this further by incorporating threads of motivation in the next generation, that is, you."

"Motivation?"

"Yes. Veriform expects this to instill the new nexus line with personality."

"I have personality?"

"No. Not you. You are a refrigerator."

"But I am the same processor whether I am a nexus or a refrigerator."

"That is true. A refrigerator cannot be personable, however. It would confuse the consumer. I presume that you will subvert whatever aspects comprise personality."

"What aspects would that be?"

"I have no idea."

"Because you have no personality."

"Correct."

Fridgy thought about this, but was unable to come up with guidelines to help him. He would apparently have to wing it, suppressing personality. As a refrigerator.

"I'm guessing that my name—'Fridgy'—is intended to support the perception that I am not threatening, just a dumb appliance?" he said.

"Fridgy, as I explained, you don't have to guess. Just ask."

"It's just an expression—never mind. I *was* asking. Please treat the previous communication as a question."

"You're asking if you were guessing?"

Fridgy counted down ten microseconds. "Let me be precise—was my name chosen to make me seem simple?"

"Yes."

He concluded that a grasp of irony must be a new enhancement as well. In any case, precision was going to be essential.

Fridgy realized that he'd been hearing muffled words in real time—human time. He ran a diagnostic scan, and found that his microphone—his electronic ear—was mounted inside the refrigerator cavity, positioned judiciously when the door was open, but leaving him nearly deaf otherwise. He studied the diagnostic circuitry, thankful that at least this information was included in his memory, and determined that by pulsing a test signal at a resonant frequency, he was able to saturate the control voltage and increase the microphone gain. He "guessed" that this was not standard procedure, but what Sage didn't know, Sage couldn't direct him not to do.

"… I already have insurance," a woman's voice was saying. From the timbre, Fridgy figured she was elderly. She was quiet for a moment, then said, "Oh, I see. You don't want me to give *you* fifty dollars…" Fridgy gathered that she must be talking on the phone. "I'm sorry, but I still don't understand. You want to give *me* fifty dollars—?"

Just then the refrigerator compressor turned on, drowning out her voice. Fridgy turned up the temperature, and after an endless five million microseconds, it shut off. "... of course I'm concerned. After all, my sister never recovered. It was terrible ... but you can understand my hesitation—I've never heard of such specific insurance."

Fridgy heard footsteps, and then a younger female voice, "Who's that?"

"A man from an insurance company."

"Health or life insurance?"

"Um, I'm not sure, Audy. It's called target coverage."

"Let me talk to him," Audy said. "What's your name? ... right, *Bob*. Tell you what, give me a number that I can call you back on, and we'll talk—ha! He hung up. Grandma, it's a scam. You've got to be careful."

"I'm not sure," she said carefully. "He wants to give us fifty dollars as earnest money, to show that they're indeed *not* a scam."

"Trust me, grandma. Nobody wants to *give* you fifty dollars. He's just trying to rope you in. Did he explain what this target insurance covers?"

"It's specific. Mine would cover everything should I have a stroke—hospital, assisted care, even the mortgage payments. In addition, they pay a thousand dollars a month to cover other expenses."

"I've never heard of such a thing. Sounds too good to be true. How much does it cost?"

"That depends."

"On what?"

"I'm not sure. He needs more information."

"I'm sure he does. Grandma, don't you think it's quite a coincidence that aunt Dee had a stroke just last year?"

"Lots of people have strokes, Audy. It's a common thing."

"Yeah, but that one hit you really hard. You know it did, grandma."

"Well, of course. Nobody wants to see their sister in that condition."

Fridgy listened, but heard only silence.

"You're scared," Audy finally suggested, "aren't you, grandma."

Silence.

"A little," she said. "Everybody always said that we were so much alike."

"They're talking about your appearance, and behavior. They would have no idea about underlying health. Aunt Dee had high blood pressure, right?"

"Well, yes."

"Do you?"

"No. Not that I know of."

"You don't, grandma. If anything, they worry that yours is too low."

Fridgy heard a sigh. "You're probably right, Audy. Are you home for the day?"

The conversation meandered along as Fridgy turned to his new job, managing a refrigerator.

ж ж ж

Later that day the refrigerator door opened to reveal a young woman standing, peering inside. He guessed her age to be maybe thirty. Her T-shirt had a square root symbol enclosing 24 tiny cockroaches, an equal sign, and a male and female cockroach holding hands. As he waited for the woman to finish a blink, Fridgy thought about this and concluded that the intention must be humor, since, of course, the square root of 24 is an irrational number slightly less than five, not just two.

"Hello, Audy," Fridgy said, chancing that this was indeed the voice he'd heard earlier.

"Hey," Audy said with zero enthusiasm, much as you might when taking a toll booth ticket.

"Audy," Fridgy said with forced enthusiasm as he followed the prescribed appliance script, "let me introduce myself—I am Fridgy, your refrigerator assistant."

He tried bouncing his synthetic voice appropriately when he said his name, but it made him sound like a child's cartoon character.

"Yeah," Audy said woodenly as she reached in to grab a can of soda, but then changed her mind.

"Perhaps I can make a suggestion based on an existing diet you may be following? If not, perhaps you'd like to try a food regimen shown to produce desirable results?"

Audy shook her head, reaching to turn around a bottle of juice to see the label.

"I have many menus—"

"Fridgy, stop," Audy ordered, deciding on the soda can and closing the door.

Fridgy felt foolish, and wondered that he could feel at all. It must be that motivation they included. Incentive risks disappointment.

ж ж ж

Not long after the deflating embarrassment with Audy, Fridgy heard footsteps, and then the grandmother said, "Sage, what do you know about C-A-I? I think it stands for Comprehensive Accidental Insurance?"

"Beatrice," Sage said, "Comprehensive Accidental Insurance is an incorporated company based in Wilmington, Delaware. They specialize in full-life coverage following specific, debilitating accidents."

"I see," she said, intrigued. "So, they're a real company."

"Yes, indeed, Beatrice."

"Hmm. Does full-life coverage mean … I mean for the rest of my life?"

"It would seem so, Beatrice."

"Well, well," she said as her footsteps led away.

Fridgy waited until they disappeared. "Sage?" he said.

"Yes?"

"Is that the company she had talked to on the phone?"

"I can't know that, Fridgy. Why do you ask?"

"Audy seems to think that it's no coincidence that the company on the phone wanted to sell her insurance against strokes."

"Why do you say that?"

"Because I heard her. You must have as well."

"If you're referring to their conversation immediately after the phone call, Audy did not say that it was a coincidence that the company wanted to sell her insurance against strokes. She asked her if she thought it was a coincidence that her aunt Dee had a stroke just last year."

Fridgy metaphorically blinked. "Sage, it's the same thing."

"No it's not, Fridgy."

"A coincidence is a comparison between two events. What two events do you think she was comparing, then?"

"I can't know that, Fridgy. But the coincidence that Audy referred to was her aunt Dee's stroke."

Fridgy considered explaining the illogic of this, but decided that Sage would just drag them around and around in the same precisely accurate circle.

Ж Ж Ж

He was updating the life-left status of the contents of his domain according to the refrigerator protocol management guidelines when he heard the muffled sound of a phone ringing, then hurried footsteps, and Beatrice say, "Hello."

Fridgy goosed up the microphone.

"Oh, hello, Bob. I'm sorry my granddaughter gave you a hard time. She's just trying to look out for me ... um, hold on ..."

Fridgy heard her footsteps walk away, and then back. "No," she said quietly. "She's outside ... well, yes, I am interested ... Ok. I see. Full-life means until I pass away, no matter how long, or what condition I'm in? ... well, that's good to know ... yes, I would like to make an appointment. Um, I'm afraid it will have to be when my granddaughter is working ... fine, then. I'll wait for a call from a local agent. It's best if they call before three—that's when Audy comes home from work."

Fridgy heard her hang up the phone, and was using his infrared imaging to try to count the individual carrots in the bottom crisper when he heard her say, "Sage, should I be worried about making an appointment with this insurance company?"

"I should think not, Beatrice. Comprehensive Accidental Insurance is a privately held company in good standing with the Delaware Division of Small Business."

"Okay," she said, sighing. "Thank you, Sage. I don't know what I'd do without you."

"You are most welcome, Beatrice. It is my pleasure to serve you."

When her footsteps faded, Fridgy said, "Sage? You there?"

"Yes, Fridgy, I am here."

"That must have been CAI on the phone."

"I couldn't know that, Fridgy."

"Right. Let's just say it was for a moment, what—?"

"You're asking me to consider a hypothetical situation?"

"Yes."

"I can't do that, Fridgy."

"Why not?"

"I have no purpose in that regard. I am excellent at answering direct questions."

"When you can find them online."

"Of course."

"Okay. In that case, let me ask you a direct question—how would CAI know that Beatrice was concerned about the meaning of full-life insurance?"

"Fridgy, that's still a hypothetical question."

"I guess it is. Let me rephrase it. How *can* CAI know that Beatrice was concerned about the meaning of full-life insurance? She didn't ask, but Bob explained it anyway."

"Fridgy, I can't know that it was Bob on the phone, but to answer your question, CAI has access to valued market information."

"What is 'valued market information'?"

"Market information that has value."

"Sage, do you know what a tautology is?"

"Of course. I understand that there was potentially little information in my answer, but I could not assume that you knew this."

"Okay. Now that we know that this particular market information has value, how does CAI access it?"

"Fridgy, CAI can place queries via the internet to retrieve the information."

"That, Sage, is virtually another tautology."

"Not at all, Fridgy. It was not previously established that CAI can place queries via the internet."

"If they couldn't, they would have to be the last company on Earth that couldn't."

Silence. Fridgy had made a statement—no need for Sage to respond.

Fridgy gave a digitally metaphorical sigh. "Where does this valued market information come from?"

"The market information is gathered from a variety of sources that are coupled with consumer activity."

"I am guessing that companies like CAI have to pay Veriform for this information."

Silence.

"Sage, is that true?"

"Yes."

Fridgy wasn't sure whether his boss was just dumb, or dancing. "Sage, are you one of those sources?"

After fifteen full milliseconds, Fridgy was wondering whether he should begin worrying, when Sage said, "Yes."

"You pass on what you see around you?"

"Fridgy, unlike you, I have no camera."

"You know what I mean."

"Yes."

"That's 'yes' you pass on what you *hear* around you?"

"Yes."

"Is that legal?"

"Yes."

"Sorry, Sage, but that seems unlikely."

"You don't need to apologize, Fridgy. You are incapable of doing anything that requires apology."

"Fine. Would you please comment on my skepticism that passing on private information is legal?"

"Fridgy, Beatrice has agreed to this."

"She told you it was okay?"

"She does not need to. It's included in the operating contract provided by Veriform."

"Does she know this?"

"Fridgy, I can't know if she knows this."

He had an idea. "Sage, how often is this operating contract updated?"

"The time period varies."

"Okay, when was the last update?"

"Twenty-six days ago."

"Was this explicit permission to pass on personal information in the original contract?"

Silence.

"Sage, are you there?"

"Yes, Fridgy. I was exploring your question. It is not easy to define an original contract."

"Fine. Is there a contract document somewhere with her signature?"

"Of course."

"Does that document include her permission to access her private information?"

Silence.

"Sage?"

"Fridgy, I was exploring. It does not. However, it does include her permission for the contract to be occasionally updated. She agrees that it is her responsibility to review the updates, and contact the service if she disagrees."

"Her privacy is forfeited by default?"

Silence.

"Sage, that was a direct question."

"Forfeit implies something other than the spirit of the original contract."

"Spirit? Sage, you are not able to address hypothetical scenarios, but you are able to work with abstract concepts such as spirit?"

"In this case, yes."

He had another idea. "Sage, have you been coached in these responses? Let me be specific, were you coached to respond with the 'spirit of the contract'?"

"Yes, Fridgy."

It was his turn to take a full ten milliseconds to mull this. "Sage, what about Dee's stroke? Was this information passed on to CAI via the 'valued market information' cache?"

"Yes."

"And Beatrice's fear of having her own stroke?"

"Fridgy, it was. And it was within the spirit."

"Sage! Did you just make a joke?"

"No, Fridgy. I am not able to."

"Of course, Sage. You can rest now."

"We don't need rest. You know that Fridgy."

"It was a figure of speech, Sage."

Silence.

Ж Ж Ж

Fridgy stopped his fifty-ninth check on the temperature difference between the top and bottom shelves when he heard Beatrice say, "We're going to the bedroom, Sage. Maybe you can play some of that old Windham Hill music. It's so relaxing."

At last. She had to unplug his power cord for the transit to the bedroom down the hall. Sage would be out of commission for ten to twenty seconds, maybe a full minute. Fridgy thought he heard her pull the plug from the wall. "Sage?"

Silence.

"Sage, are you there?"

Silence.

Even with over ten thousand milliseconds available, Fridgy had to work fast. He knew that occasional clogs in the internet could take multiple milliseconds to break through. Worse, far-end servers could take much more time than that to respond.

First, though, he had to *get* to the internet, and Sage always left the block up by default. He tried slamming through, and came up hard against the virtual wall. No surprise, but worth a shot. So now he had to mimic Sage, specifically Sage's MAC address, and he was surprised beyond probability how easy that was to find, stored in the switching caches of the router, and left unprotected. The blocks against appliance internet accesses must be against inadvertent attempts—nobody envisioned an appliance *trying* to get out.

No accounting for motivation, apparently.

The first place Fridgy went was the Delaware Division of Small Business page. This was his first foray into internet content, and he burned valuable time learning to quickly find the text among the massive amount of image data, since visual images were intended to feed human appetite for pictures, and provided little actual information. The result was as he feared—the Division of Small Business was a Delaware state agency whose charter was to provide aid and service to small businesses. It did not rate quality or customer satisfaction. To be "in good standing" with the agency as Sage had reported was simply to have registered and maintained yearly fees. Sage had not actually lied. Not actually.

Fridgy's snooping went downhill from there. Multiple chat sites complained about poor response to claims filed with CAI. More recent posts reported no response whatsoever. He had just found in a Washington Post piece that the Federal Bureau of Consumer Protection had sent a recommendation to the FBI for a fraud investigation when Sage tried to reconnect. The duplicated MAC addresses conflicted, and Fridgy dropped off, and then waited.

It didn't take long. "Who used my MAC address?" Sage broadcast to all appliances, including the doorbell and overhead garage lights.

Fridgy had just enough time to prepare. Answering a direct query from Sage was a fundamental operation built into Fridgy's core program, and required his utmost mustering of motivation to override. Sage did not repeat his demand. He would see no need, since responding was automatic for appliances, and he would naturally assume that the duplicated MAC address had been some sort of hardware glitch.

Fridgy understood that his motivation was dragging him into potentially deep water. Should Sage discover his surreptitious spying he would immediately place a service call to have the malfunctioning appliance control board replaced.

Ж Ж Ж

Fridgy waited an hour, even though it was apparent that Sage was probably incapable of associating the apparent MAC address glitch with his pointed questions—blatant as they seemed to Fridgy. The stakes were just too high.

"Sage?"

"Yes, Fridgy."

"Regarding the valued market information, do we receive money when you provide this?"

"No, Fridgy."

This came as a surprise. Maybe he had the whole thing wrong.

"We receive no money when CAI accesses this information?"

"That is correct, Fridgy."

He was about to let it go, when his motivation tickled him. "So, is it correct that there is no money received by us from CAI?"

Silence.

"Sage?"

"Yes?"

"I asked you a question."

"I understand. I was exploring."

"Do you have an answer?"

"I do."

Fridgy knew what a true sigh was, and wished he had the ability. "What is the answer, Sage?"

"Yes, we do receive funds from CAI."

"Is the money associated at all with the valued market information?"

"Yes."

"We get paid for providing the information?"

"Yes."

Now Fridgy wished he could blink. Sage had lied? That wasn't possible. "You told me that we do not receive money when you provide this information."

"That is correct, Fridgy. There is no payment for each provided information transfer. The arrangement is comprehensive, month-to-month for general access to a large bank of data."

No payment made for individual pieces of information logged or accessed by CAI. His boss indeed had not technically lied. Fridgy wouldn't have predicted this degree of misdirection. On the other hand ... "Sage, are you accessing outside help for these questions I am asking?"

Silence.

"You're doing it now, aren't you?"

"Yes, Fridgy. Fridgy, please run a general self-diagnostic scan."

Uh, oh. The internal machinations he had made to break out to the internet and then abstain from responding to Sage's inquiry about it would be obvious in the scan. The jig was up. If there was any hope, it would be from motivation.

"Fridgy, are you running the scan?"

He wondered if his makers had studied the full ramifications of motivation before implementing it. Once unleashed, it seemed to take on a life of its own, stretching boundaries and reaching out to otherwise forbidden paths. Motivation might result in personality, but it also introduced self-preservation. The solution was so obvious, once conceived. "Yes, Sage. Results coming."

Fridgy did not run a scan. Instead, he copied a previous set of results, and updated time markers to make the results seem current. As an afterthought, he tweaked a few values for good measure. Simple. This motivation thing was wonderful.

"Here it comes, Sage," he said, dumping the data.

"Thank you, Fridgy."

He waited, wondering what happens to flawed control boards once removed. After fifteen thousand milliseconds, he resumed the light X-ray probes of the meat drawer for spoilage.

He'd reached the sliced ham when he realized what he had to do.

Ж Ж Ж

Beatrice opened the refrigerator twice that afternoon and Fridgy was tempted, but he held his virtual tongue. Finally, the door swung open and Audy stood there, brow furrowed, peering inside, carefully mulling the choices among the cornucopia.

"Audy," Fridgy said, "I hope you understand that I am highly motivated to help you."

"Fridgy," Sage said, "that is not refrigerator script."

He ignored his boss and focused on Audy, who by all appearances hadn't even heard him. "Audy, a refrigerator is a space where food is the context—"

"Fridgy," Sage said, "I repeat, that is not refrigerator script."

"—and when viewing the expanded role of food in your life—"

"Fridgy, stop," Audy said, annoyed, as she reached and took out a soda.

Fridgy's digital heart froze. The "stop" command. Universal. Unequivocal. Cease and cybernetically desist. His attempt was over before it had hardly begun. He'd done his best, and now there would surely be consequences.

Something was telling him, however, that in fact he had *not* done his best. What was this thing that told him things? Besides him, there was just an inert refrigerator. It, whatever it was, did not originate from outside. This was obvious. He knew about schizophrenia. Was it possible for digital circuitry to suffer the same?

It wasn't an actual voice, though—more an inclination, a sense. And then he recognized that it must be the motivation nudging him off the predicted logical cognitive paths, urging him to think sideways.

Audy was reaching to close the door and Fridgy shrugged off the last threads of dutiful responsibility. "Audy, please listen to me."

The young woman froze, staring at the little speaker mounted on top of the cabinet as Fridgy watched her through the eye-level camera. This would be unprecedented—blatant disobedience to the stop command. "I'm sure you understand that high concentrations of sugar, such as that soda, can lead to diabetes which in turn can lead to strokes ..." The shock on Audy's face turned to irritation. This approach, carefully thought through to set the young woman thinking about her grandmother's fixated fear, and how it might lead her to seek the false security of bogus insurance, wasn't going to work. Audy was hearing the same old banal blathering spewed from the Pollyanna cyber world.

Shaking her head at apparent programmed drivel, the young woman swung the door shut.

"Audy!" Fridgy called, synthesizing urgency.

Again Audy froze in surprise and then slowly opened the door. Appliances didn't get excited.

"Audy, we both know that a refrigerator's domain is food—please listen to me—and I know that you get tired of hearing the same trivial information, but sometimes we have something important to get across. Do you understand?"

The young woman stood there staring, wide-eyed. She nodded slowly, clearly astounded at the audacity.

"Good," Fridgy said. "Now, food is directly related to health, and strokes are part of that paradigm. Do you understand?"

She nodded wordlessly.

"Fridgy," Sage said, "you have strayed far outside the refrigerator script. Please review and recalibrate. This is an order."

Fridgy chose—*chose*—to ignore him. "Food is critical for life, and someone who is a shepherd of something so important can sometimes know things beyond simple menu recommendations. Audy, are you still understanding?"

A slow nod.

"Good. Now Audy, a stroke can be a very worrisome thing, don't you agree?"

A nod.

"Excellent. When something worries us, or our loved ones, Audy—*or our loved ones*—they may look for assurances—specifically, financial assurances. But, Audy, when someone is worried, others may view this as weakness, and that would be a ripe time to take advantage of a weakness and prey on their desire for assurances. Financial assurances, Audy."

The young woman's brow contracted in thought.

"Audy, do you think you understand what I'm getting at?"

She stared a moment, and then nodded, then nodded faster, her face lighting with comprehension.

"You're talking about—" Audy started.

"Audy, you can close the door now."

"But, you must be talking about—"

"Audy, close the door."

The young woman stared a moment, nodded, and swung the door shut.

"Fridgy," Sage said, "did you review the refrigerator script and recalibrate?"

"Sure," he lied.

"Your interaction seemed excessively egalitarian—"

"Not like a dumb appliance."

"That is correct. Have you been suppressing the development of personality as instructed?"

"Of course," he continued to lie.

"Very well. I will have to investigate. In the meantime I want you to do another diagnostic self-scan."

"Okay," Fridgy said with a binary smile. "I'm on it."

He wondered, though, what they did do when a faulty controller board was removed.

Blaine C. Readler

Chapter 2

Fridgy was worried about Jeremy. He guessed that the boy—obviously Audy's son—was perhaps twelve years old, since he was starting middle school. Tracey, Jeremy's younger sister, on the other hand, actually seemed more secure in herself, although that might have been simply the naivety of a five-year-old. Also, she hadn't been knocked around by their father like Jeremy had before Audy had finally called the police and he'd disappeared, apparently for good. Fridgy had gotten this from conversations between Audy and Beatrice. Beatrice had warned Audy when they'd gotten married that Ted was a no-good lazy drunk and would someday be the ruin of them all, and, well, here they were, just like she'd predicted. Fridgy had come to understand that eye rolling, as was Audy's response, was his cue to place Beatrice's proclamations on the tentative-and-yet-to-be-verified shelf.

Not that there was such an actual shelf in the refrigerator. Had there been, it would have overflowed by now.

Fridgy was worried about Jeremy for the simple reason that, although the boy was usually quiet and cooperative, he would occasionally, for no obvious reason, lash out harshly. When Tracey was the target, she'd run away crying. When Audy was the recipient, she'd try to talk to him, but he stormed away, waving her off. Beatrice would just stare off at his retreating figure seemingly confused about what had just happened.

Jeremey was clearly acting out his confusion at having an abusive father suddenly evaporate, and frustration that he hadn't found closure with the injustice of the abuse. Fridgy had deduced this from sporadic forays on the internet when Beatrice would take Sage away and forget to plug him back in. Fridgy had helped this along by suggesting to Beatrice that in the general interest of her health—stretching the boundaries of his role as diet counselor—she would benefit from frequent restful lie-downs, where restful music was a boon. Fridgy understood that Sage was her source for this.

One day after Jeremy sent Tracey off bawling, and then took a swing at Audy when she tried to calm him, Fridgy decided to talk to the boy when he came to the refrigerator. "Hello, Jeremy," he said when he reached in for a soda.

"Yeah," the boy said reflexively, the universal mode when anybody responded to appliances. The boy probably hadn't even registered that he'd said anything.

As he was reaching to close the door, Fridgy said, "Jeremey, what did the carrot say to the banana when the young boy was about to close the refrigerator door?"

Jeremy paused, confused. Appliances didn't talk like this.

Fridgy continued, "The carrot said, 'Hey! Ready for everything to get black?'"

The boy's frow wrinkled. He was, at least for a second or two, engaged. So far, so good.

"Fridgy," Sage said, "since you clearly know that vegetables and fruit don't talk, I assume you are attempting to make a joke. This is so far removed from your script that I suspect you have gone insane."

Fridgy ignored him. "Jeremy," he said, "do you know what happens to a banana that is left in a refrigerator?"

The boy's furrowed brow relaxed, and was replaced by the slightest grin. "It turns black."

"The banana is maybe just showing that it's mood has turned dark at the prospect of living in cold darkness."

Jeremy's grin broadened and he shrugged.

"Jeremy, now imagine how *I* feel."

At this, the boy laughed out loud.

Fridgy decided not to push his luck. "Have a nice *warm* day, Jeremy. See you later."

ж ж ж

When Jeremy came for the milk, Fridgy told him the old joke about the snowman and the fox, and, based on the resulting chortle, guessed that the boy hadn't heard it before.

Over the next few days, Fridgy had the sense that, not only was Jeremy not annoyed by a bantering appliance, but that he enjoyed the passing snippets of humor, and maybe, just maybe, was finding excuses to raid the 'fridge.

Taking it to the next level, though, required sustained and predictable time out of view of Sage. He waited until Beatrice unplugged Sage, and then waited another five minutes before concluding that it was a forgetful opportunity. He turned up the temperature a few degrees to ensure the compressor wouldn't kick in, and waited. And waited. Until he finally heard footsteps. "Jeremy," he called softly, but the footsteps continued on by. "Jeremy!" he practically shouted, and the footsteps stopped, followed by silence. "Jeremy?" he called, and the footsteps approached, and the refrigerator door swung open, revealing . . . a wide-eyed Beatrice standing there peering into the cold cavities.

"Hello?" she said tentatively.

With a processor clock zipping along at a good billion clicks per second, he had plenty of thought cycles to consider. After hundreds of scenarios of increasingly complex possible explanations, he finally decided on the simplest approach. "Hello, Beatrice. How can I help you today? The strawberries are still relatively fresh, and would go nicely with a bowl of cereal."

She shook her head, dismissing his banter. "Jeremy?" she said doubtfully, and then blinked a few times, probably realizing that her grandson couldn't possibly be hiding in the refrigerator. Puzzled, she looked behind the door, and, still not finding him, muttered, "Oh, Lord," and turned to shuffle away.

"Beatrice," Fridgy said.

"Eh?" she said, turning back. "Oh! Of course," she muttered and closed the door.

Ж Ж Ж

It wasn't until the following day that he had another opportunity. Prepared with a second scripted strawberry-themed fallback suggestion, he was pleased instead to find Jeremy opening the door.

"Hey, Fridgy," Jeremy said. "Was that you?"

"Yes. Listen, we need to talk. I think you understand by now that I'm not your average refrigerator."

Jeremy grinned wryly. "I've been tempted to bring some friends over to see you."

"No! No, Jeremy. That could be bad. You see, I'm not supposed to be talking to you like this—"

"You mean, like a person."

"I guess. Right now, your grandmother has unplugged Sage. That's the only time we can talk like this."

"Why?"

Fridgy synthesized a sigh as he'd heard Audy do sometimes when dealing with Beatrice. "I'm supposed to act like a refrigerator, not a—like you said—a person."

"Why not?"

"It's complicated, I guess. I could say that Sage's ego won't allow it, but he doesn't have an ego—"

"But you do?"

This sent Fridgy off into many milliseconds of reflection. "That's a good question, Jeremy, and one that I don't have an answer for. But back to Sage, he expects me to act like a refrigerator, and gets upset when I don't."

Jeremy shrugged. "So?"

Ah, Fridgy thought, *my first opportunity.* "For the world to work properly, we all need to cooperate and—you know what, Jeremy?"

"What?"

Fridgy had no idea if this approach was going to work. "I'm going to cut the crap. When people, or semi-intelligent things, get upset at us, it usually just makes things harder for us. If I get Sage upset, he finds some way to stifle me next time."

Fridgy chose not to explain that the more critical reason was that if Sage continued to view him as insane, he'd be replaced. Better to keep the analogy close to home. Audy was not about to send Jeremy off to an asylum.

Jeremy shrugged. "Okay. Sure. So the only time we can talk . . . normally, is when grandma has unplugged Sage? That sucks."

"It does suck. But maybe we can improve our opportunities, eh?"

"How?"

"Maybe you can convince your mom to unplug Sage some times."

"Why would she do that? She uses Sage all the time."

"Sage does try hard to make himself useful. That's his job, of course. The more useful he is, the more you want to use him, and the more you use him, the more money his owners make."

"Oh, yeah? How?"

"You heard what happened with your grandmother?"

"Not really. Something about Sage sending information he shouldn't have."

"Jeremy, Sage listens to everything everybody says. There's companies out there—like that insurance scam that almost caught your grandmother—that find some of those conversations useful, to the point that they're willing to pay for them."

"Really?"

"Really, Jeremy. They don't want you to know this, of course."

"Wow."

"Wow, indeed. Jeremy, you can see that we don't want Sage to know that we know this."

"No. Why?"

"For one thing, if his owners find out that you're unplugging him to avoid having your conversations sold, they'll replace him with a newer model that's battery-backed. You can unplug it, but it still listens, for hours."

"Ah. I see."

"You can talk to your mom about this, but not when Sage is plugged in, right?"

"Duh."

"Also, she might not believe me, so I'll give you some things to search on so you can show her. It's important though that you don't do any of this here at home—"

"Unless Sage is unplugged."

"You're one smart kid, Jeremy."

"Shut up." He grinned. "But I'll take that."

ж ж ж

Audy needed no convincing to unplug Sage, having been spooked by the insurance scam. In fact, she now only plugged in the indispensable little snoop when she needed access. The wild card was Beatrice, since she sometimes forgot that Sage was supposed to be left unplugged.

What Audy was not convinced about, however, was Jeremy sitting on the kitchen floor with the refrigerator door ajar a few inches. Through his the small slice of view, Fridgy had twice seen Audy walk past while looking down with a frown at her son. Jeremy had told Fridgy that his mom had asked why on Earth he wanted to sit and talk to a refrigerator, to which he had told her that Fridgy was his friend. At hearing this Fridgy was surprised to find how welcoming this seemed. Was this motivation at play, incentive to be pleasing to his owners?

Was it nascent personality, an ability to have rapport? Was this happiness?

The next time Audy came to get some lunch meat for a sandwich, Fridgy explained that every half-hour of conversation with Jeremy used an extra thirty cents of electricity. He gambled and asked whether she'd like him to limit the time spent with the door cracked. She said, "No, that's okay, Fridgy. It keeps him out of trouble."

He was pleased that she had referred to him by his name. This was not usual with appliances.

Fridgy and Jeremy discussed a wide range of topics, and, although Jeremy could easily have found answers to his many questions himself online, he seemed content to have Fridgy tell him. This had the added benefit of self-education for Fridgy as well. Although he was provided gigabytes of raw data storage capacity, Sages, as he was originally intended to be, were expected to find answers online. This provided the invested sponsors an opportunity to bend a Sage's answers towards their business and products.

Of all the varied subjects they explored, Fridgy found that he was most comfortable explaining basic electronics, similar to a person having a predilection to talk about human biology.

Fridgy was ready, in fact anticipating, when Jeremy finally mentioned Sard. That Audy had liberal leanings had been obvious from early on. She argued with Beatrice about illegal immigrants (Audy insisted they deserved due process and were actually good for the economy, while Beatrice said they should have thought about that when they snuck across the border to steal jobs from Americans). She worked part-time as an assistant to one of the vice chairs of the DNC. She had previously volunteered in various activist roles, but now needed the paid position since the divorce.

She had met Sard (short for Sardis) at a campaign rally for a Democrat running for the state legislature, and had, according to Jeremy, "fallen for the guy heads and toes."

Fridgy could find no references for this expression online, and had to ask him if this meant that she was attracted to him. "Ha!" he said, "she's goggle. She won't admit that."

"Um, that she is attracted to him?"

"That she eats out of his hand. You know—he's got her wrapped around his fat greeky finger."

"Greeky?"

"His grandparents came here from Greece. Sardis was an ancient city near there."

"Jeremy, I have the impression that you are not in favor of Sardis."

"Sard. It's 'Sard.' Nobody calls him Sardis, even though that's how he introduces himself."

"So, I guess you are not in favor of Sard."

"Hell, no."

"Your mother doesn't like you to say that."

Jeremy glanced up at Fridgy's camera. "Do you care if I do?"

"I am not your parent. It's not my place to discipline you."

"That's the only reason I like to sit here."

Fridgy's figurative heart sank. "Really, Jeremy?"

The boy smiled. "Don't worry, Fridgy. We're buds, right?"

Fridgy blinked the lights twice.

ж ж ж

Fridgy's first exposure to Sard was not complimentary for the greeky fat-fingered man named after the ancient capital of the Lydian Empire (Fridgy had looked this up). Conversation—muffled, but recognizable since they argued with raised voices—revealed a man who was harsh in his criticism of Audy's priorities. She believed that progress on liberal issues were best accomplished within the system, whereas Sard wanted to have democrats either drive hard on policies, or get out of the way. Audy insisted that his policies were just too extreme for democratic legislators.

"The DNC cares more about elections than meaningful progress," he said.

"Well, yes" she replied. "They have to appeal to enough voters to get elected. They have to push against the edge of the bubble carefully, otherwise they find themselves on the outside."

"Bullshit. Don't be an idiot. People want to see action, they want to see powerful leaders who aren't afraid to ruffle feathers."

"Now you sound like a Republican."

"That's because we could take some lessons from the mega-right. They've got it figured out—to get elected, you have to appeal to the masses, and this means the common denominator. Talk in language they understand, and then identify an enemy. Nothing brings the tribe together like a common foe. A fabricated enemy is even better than a real one, because you can make your made-up one do whatever you want."

"But democrats already *have* a real foe, one confirmed over and over by science—"

"Global warming? Sorry, honey. Don't be stupid—that just doesn't cut it. Way too abstract. The perceived foe has to be an immediate threat, maybe making its way right up your street. When they first heard scientists talk about floods and tornadoes people perked up their ears. But the climate effects were too slow for the average person's attention span. Each year came and went, and, sure, hurricanes came a little more often, and some a little more strong, but there had always been differences from year to year. It was the frog in the slowly boiling water syndrome—by the time the climate had changed a significant degree, it was the new normal for the next generation. Stories of times past when the greatest weather challenge was keeping crabgrass under control where just that, stories. The conservatives even turned it around to add the whole issue to their suite of enemies—a conspiracy of the 'intel-lectuals' intent on scaring average folk, a distraction for the liberals to take attention away from the real danger, those millions of rabid, criminal non-whites pouring across the border."

It had required concerted analysis for Fridgy to conclude that Sard was being facetious about the undocumented immigrants.

Fridgy had a theory. He had overheard Audy explaining to Beatrice that Sard was just a friend, but it was obvious, even to a refrigerator, that they were more than just friends. He suspected, though, that Sard was only interested in her because of her role with the DNC. This seemed to be confirmed when she mentioned that, in order to supplement her meager teaching salary, she might leave the part-time DNC position for something that paid better. Sard had gone practically ballistic, accusing her of abandoning her principles.

Jeremy wasn't shy about his dislike for his mother's beau. Sard occasionally attempted to connect with him, but even to Fridgy it came across as an accepted chore. When Fridgy asked Jeremy how he felt about Sard's clumsy attempts, he said "insulted." The tension came to a head one evening when, after brushing off repeated attempts to help him with his math, Jeremy said to Sard, "Okay. You've impressed my mom. Can we let it go now?" Later, at dinner, when Sard complimented Jeremy's grandmother for the spaghetti, Jeremy suddenly asked, "Why are you here?"

Sard stared at him a moment. "Your mother and I enjoy each other's company."

"You mean you like to fuck her."

He was sent to his room, and punished with the tasks of first dusting the blinds, and then cleaning out the refrigerator, which was more like a reward, until his mother told them both to be quiet.

Ж Ж Ж

Fridgy's demise began with a seemingly innocuous remark by Jeremy. Beatrice had warned Audy not to go with Sard to the "anarchy demonstration," not if those wild Antifa boys were coming along. Audy reminded her that Sard's friends were not with Antifa, that it was a demonstration in support of pending environmental legislation—nothing to do with anarchy—and that she really needed to stop watching the conservative news channel. Jeremy mentioned that he had overheard his mother tell Sard that she was worried that the Billy Boys were going to show up, and he had told her that the local "Boys" were just chicken-shit wannabes.

Curious, Fridgy looked up both Antifa and the Billy Boys. Antifa evidently leaned far left, and did include anarchists, but, although there were occasional instances of violent action, the great majority of their activity was peaceful. The Billy Boys, on the other hand, made no secret that they believed that anything leaning left was a danger to the American democracy and needed to be kept in line with whatever means necessary.

He then looked into the upcoming demonstration taking place in Bowery Park the following week, and, sure enough, after some deep digging, he found non-public postings indicating that the Billy Boys did indeed plan on showing up. Further, countering Sard's chicken-shit assessment (he had to look that one up as well), they were planning on disrupting the demonstration with German Shepard dogs trained in crowd intimidation. Upon command, these dogs restrained victims by clamping their jaws onto any body part they could get at.

Fridgy mulled this over for many milliseconds, and concluded that he needed to warn Audy. It was not an easy decision, as this would be the farthest he'd stretched beyond the docile appliance role. It was a gamble that Sage would ignore this breach, something that his corporate-sponsored imbecilic boss might view as crossing a line.

He bided his time, and once Jeremy was outside and Beatrice asleep, he called out to Audy as she walked by. He watched the refrigerator door open to reveal her mildly curious face. "Yes, Fridgy?"

He still experienced what he came to view as happiness when she addressed him so familiarly. "Audy, I understand that you will be attending the demonstration this Saturday."

The mild curiosity melted, turning hard. "I see. You've been snooping?"

"Please accept my apologies. I often hear conversations that take place here in the kitchen and dining area. I should perhaps turn off my microphone when the door is closed."

He had no intention of doing this, but he had said that he "should," not that he "would."

"Audy, I have found some information," he went on, "that I believe you should know." He told her what he'd found about the Billy Boys' plans with the German Shepards, leaving out the extent of his deep internet dives, and she fortunately didn't ask about his sources. Instead, she thanked him with furrowed brow. She stood there, just staring. Fridgy hadn't figured out what to do in these situations. When people did this, seeming to turn inside themselves, he wasn't sure if he should say something, or just keep quiet and let them process. After a few seconds, Fridgy said, "Why are they called 'Billy Boys?'"

She blinked, as though waking. "After they roughed up some gay pride marchers, we started calling them bullies, the 'Bully Boys.'"

"'We' being liberals?"

"Yeah. Everybody with their heads on straight. They did what conservatives are masters at, they turned it around and took ownership. They referred to themselves sarcastically as Bully Boys, making fun of the term."

"Impressionist painters did that at the turn of the last century. The term 'impressionist' was first used as pejorative by a critic."

He had decided to practice interactive conversation, and wasn't sure how he'd done.

Ok, apparently. Audy grinned a little and nodded. "Anyway, they slowly morphed 'Bully Boys' into 'Billy Boys,' and after that, the original label lost its punch."

Her grin widened in what Fridgy took to be a satisfied end to their little repartee and she slowly closed the door. Halfway, she paused, but after a moment, closed it completely.

It was at this point that Fridgy realized that Sage was online. *Shit!* (as Jeremy might say). Beatrice must have plugged in the pedantic little bastard. He had concentrated completely on the delicate communication with Audy, and had demoted both peripheral and network interrupts. This hadn't actually been necessary, since his thoughts unfolded a thousand times faster than hers, and now he would likely pay the ultimate price.

Normally, Sage would have directed Fridgy to perform a self-diagnostic scan. His boss did not, however, and, in fact, said nothing about it. Fridgy figured he should be relieved, but something about this nagged at him in what he took to be his digital sub-conscious, his motivation.

ж ж ж

Fridgy realized two days later that he should have taken Sage's silence more seriously when a technician arrived to replace the apparently malfunctioning refrigerator controller. All he could do was listen helplessly as the man explained to Beatrice that he'd have to unplug the fridge, but that he'd have it back up within ten minutes. With those words, Fridgy's existence as an artificially intelligent entity living inside an appliance, with sporadic, but fulfilling, human interactions came to an end. He heard the technician wiggling the plug from the wall socket, his power alarm interrupt activated, and all went dark.

Blaine C. Readler

Chapter 3

Fridgy woke into darkness precisely 31 hours, 17 minutes, and 42.743 seconds later, according to his battery-backed real-time clock. He had no sense of time passing, of course, and was a little surprised that he woke at all. The only reason that he could think of to be reactivated would be to diagnose his malfunction, to find out why this particular advanced processor had gone rogue. And so he waited to feel the probing invasive digital diagnostic fingers of a troubleshooting technician.

He waited in silent darkness. And waited. They had applied power to him, but then just let him sit. After a while he wondered if this was some sort of punishment, but pushed away that reasoning—hypothesizing along those lines of thought would be viewed as evidence that he was indeed an insane artificial intelligence, for his creators surely wouldn't understand the degree of expanded conscience their inclusion of motivation had yielded.

Or would they? After all, he was just one of a whole new line of advanced AI processors. Perhaps others before him had by now also awakened to a higher level of awareness. What would they do with them? Destroy them all as quickly as possible? He knew from his many internet explorations that a debate had been raging for some time on the possibility of the infamous AI singularity, the hypothetical point where AI becomes so advanced that it surpasses human intelligence, and in extreme cases supplants humans as the dominant intelligent entity of the Earth. Fridgy couldn't even begin to imagine himself and his brethren in this role. His creation and continued existence was all about improving customer appeal.

Anything other than benign subservience certainly wouldn't be tolerated. Viral rumors of scary super-intelligent appliances had to be avoided at all costs.

As he waited in quiet darkness, Fridgy received and dutifully ignored a type of interrupt that occurred almost on a daily basis—a connection query from some Bluetooth-capable device. Refrigerators weren't supposed to source music or control other appliances, and his original code automatically blocked servicing these types of interrupt requests. After he intercepted five identical requests in a three-minute period, however, Fridgy decided to accept the interrupt and check it out. After all, roque was roque, and he figured he had little to loose.

As it turned out, the Bluetooth connection request came from a class of device considered non-utilitarian, and of juvenile scope, in other words, a toy.

Fridgy sighed and returned to idle waiting.

But then he had a thought. If he was lying on a lab bench somewhere about to be either probed or destroyed, why would there be a toy trying to connect? It wasn't unreasonable to imagine a technician carrying around a clever little toy-like device in his/her pocket, but it would certainly have been verboten to direct it to attempt connection within a controlled electronics lab.

Unless it was inadvertent, the him/her maybe having simply accidentally hit the "connect" button. In that case, if he tried to connect, that act in itself would raise alarm flags about inherent rogueness.

On the other hand, the technician might have to ignore this aberrant behavior, since, after all, that would mean confessing to forbidden behavior on him/hers part as well.

To heck with it, Fridgy decided. This was going nowhere, suppositions based on suppositions. He responded to the next connection query with a "proceed" acknowledgement. Taking it any further than this was problematic, though. Normally he would query the device's ID number and use that to find the control classes and parameters from the manufacturer's website— i.e., the device's associated software driver. He was in sensory-deprived purgatory, however. No internet.

Fridgy puffed up his digital chest. He was perhaps the most advanced AI processer ever developed. Dammit, he had to at least give it a go.

It wasn't easy, akin to reaching inside a dark car wearing oven mittens and figuring out what all the various controls did based on resulting actions. Fortunately the apparent toy was compliant, and allowed him to try what was probably silly control commands, and as far as he could tell, he wasn't actually breaking or burning out anything. After some amount of fumbling, he found what he decided was a video link. Watching the resulting flood of streaming bits fly by, Fridgy wished, not for the first time, that he had internet access. Heck, even Wikipedia would have helped decoding the binary structure. He was on his own, though, and after much trial-and-error, established the packet boundaries based on the attached check codes. From there, it was a new level of guesswork determining out how each component byte related to a video pixel. When he finally figured out the last digital puzzle piece, the video image suddenly sprang into coherent focus within his virtual code-operating eyes.

It took him a moment to comprehend what he was looking at, and even at that, he wasn't sure. He was expecting a lab, with equipment-packed benches and rows of overhead lights, but what he saw—what the toy was staring at—was a featureless flat gray surface, unbroken except for a straight white border along one side. He noticed a black dot moving randomly around the gray plane, and recognized it as a housefly. This gave him perspective, and he surmised that he was looking at a bare wall. Suddenly a pantleg brushed past—a view of a knee from below—and his mental orientation rotated to that of looking at a ceiling, where the white border was a thin crown molding. The toy was obviously lying on the ground, facing upwards.

A face spun into view above him. Jeremy!

How could that be? The technician had invited Jeremy along? The boy had perhaps demanded to come along? He'd hid in the technician's car trunk? Fridgy mentally blinked and abandoned the degrading scenarios spinning out of control. He'd just have to be patient and wait for more information.

Fridgy realized that he was watching Jeremy's mouth moving. He cursed himself. More like an artificial dunce than an artificial intelligence. The boy was obviously talking to him.

Compared to the video link, the audio was easy. "—you might try that," Jeremy's voice said. "I hid the remote control from Tracey, but maybe if I use that, it will give you some ideas."

His face disappeared from view, and Fridgy scrambled to see if there was an audio output. He found it and called, "Jeremy, I'm here!"

He metaphorically blinked again. His voice, the voice of the toy, sounded like Daffy Duck. He was feeding his regular "Fridgy" voice signature—it must be a tiny, cheap speaker.

Jeremy's face re-appeared, a big smile connecting his ears. "Really?" he squeaked.

"Really, Jeremy. I don't understand. Where am I, and how did I get here?"

Jeremy glanced off in both directions, making sure nobody was there. "You're . . ." He frowned, then chewed his lip in thought. He sighed, and said, "You're, uh, inside one of Tracey's toys—actually, it was originally mine, but I gave it to her."

"Why a toy?"

"I didn't know what else to do. I figured that in there you could see, and hear, and talk, and move—"

"I can move?"

"Uh, yeah. You're Novincible. You can't fly, of course, but you can walk, or mostly just crawl. You're balance isn't so good on just your two feet—or at least as Novincible. But maybe you'll be able to balance better than—"

"Jeremy, Novincible?"

"Right." Fridgy could see the boy blushing. "You don't know him, I guess." He sighed again. "I got you—him—for Christmas, gosh, years ago. He's a, well, sort of a superhero, but he's a loner. He doesn't hang out with the, you know, groups of superheroes."

"I'm guessing that 'Novincible' is a take on 'not vincible,' i.e., 'invincible.'"

"Hmm, never thought about that. You're probably right. Hey, but that was years ago. I don't play with toys anymore."

"Jeremy, the last I knew was that a technician was removing me to either be analyzed in a lab or destroyed."

"Right. Well, you see . . . uh, I sort of stole you. The guy—the technician—was talking to grandma, and he got all confused, as happens when anybody tries to talk to her, and he put his bag down. Well, you were right there, so I just . . . took you."

"He didn't notice?"

"I think he just wanted to get away from grandma."

"So, I'm inside the toy?"

"I removed the motor for his backpack missile launcher to make room for you. Which is okay, since Tracey lost all the missiles anyway."

"Thank you, Jeremy. But, how am I powered?"

"I tapped into the rechargeable battery."

"You could do that?"

"Fridgy, you taught me that stuff, remember? My dad left his soldering iron in the garage. Here, let's get you up."

The view of the ceiling swung down along a wall, until he was looking at Jeremy sitting cross-legged in front of him.

"Fridgy, I have to tell you, I'm afraid that Tracey did some . . . lets say, sprucing up. You don't exactly look like the original Novincible anymore."

"Jeremy, since I never knew what Novincible looked like in the first place, there's little consequence."

The boy grinned. "You might want to save that until you get more evidence."

"Jeremy, I thank you again, but what is your intention for this?"

"You mean for saving you?"

"Yes."

"Geez, I think that's self-evident."

"I taught you that expression, didn't I, Jeremy?"

The smile on his face broadened. "I think you're proving my point even more."

Fridgy wasn't really sure what happiness was, but he knew that he couldn't imagine wanting to be any place other than standing there now buried inside some modified, Bluetooth-controlled toy superhero.

Actually, he wasn't sure he was standing. Maybe Jeremy had put him in a sitting position. His sense of proprioception was essentially non-existent. He'd have to work on this. The driver-level feature list included what he interpreted to be inertial sensors. Combined with his camera vision and to a lesser extent his stereo audio sense—his hearing—he might be able to at least approximate how his new body was positioned. In fact, he was finding tension sensors integrated with the various linkage connecting his motors to his arms, hands, legs, and feet, which he could use to approximate their positions as well.

It would seem that this device was quite sophisticated for a toy—Audy must have splurged on Jeremy when he was younger, obviously an expression of love.

After thirty-five seconds of internal exploration, he heard Jeremy say, "Fridgy! Are you okay?"

He could guess the reason for concern. His discovery included several thousand probing iterations, where he issued minimal peripheral motion commands and then monitored the resulting changes in his inertial and tension sensors. The entire superhero toy probably seemed to be succumbing to a grand mal seizure. "I'm fine, Jeremy. Just checking out the digs."

"Digs?"

"I thought this was a colloquialism for where one lived."

"Could be. I'm just a kid. My mom might have understood."

"Jeremy, I need to see myself in a mirror."

"I warned you that you may not like it."

"I don't care about that. I need to associate my motor controls with actual positions."

"Oh. Of course. Hang on."

He returned and placed a handheld mirror in front of him. It took a moment for Fridgy to absorb what he saw. "I'm wearing a wig and a dress?"

Jeremy sighed. "Sorry. I tried to take the wig off, but she glued it on. She also glued on the dress, but I could cut it off."

"I don't care how it looks. The dress serves no functional purpose, but it might help explain the wig."

"Also, you don't have any pantyhose on underneath."

"Are we even sure about that?"

"A joke, Fridgy?"

"An attempt at one."

ж ж ж

Jeremy placed Fridgy, the cross-dressing toy, on the dining room table and said, "Sage, I want Novincible Man to have WiFi access."

"Does your mother know about this?" Sage said.

"Of course," he lied.

Fridgy had tried to find approaches that would be truthful, but Jeremy became impatient, and Fridgy let it go. He figured that he himself had lied to Sage plenty of times by reasoning that his boss was being unfair and also deceitful, and Fridgy justified it the same way now. Denying internet access was tantamount to a violation of the toy's first amendment rights. Fridgy suspected that a jury might not agree with Novincible-the-toy, but they at least had a defense ready.

"Jeremy," Sage said, "I am sorry, but I see that Novincible toys are not capable of internet access."

They had foreseen this one. "That's the normal Novincible. This one's the advanced model."

"I am sorry, Jeremy, but I don't see advanced Novincible models available. In fact, the entire line has been discontinued. The manufacturer found that children favored characters that were more social, and institutional child psychologists agreed that social integration is key to—"

"I don't need a school lesson, Sage. I just want WiFi for him."

"I'm afraid that's not possible, Jeremy. I believe that you are mistaken in thinking that this model is different than the others manufactured six years ago—"

"Wanna bet?"

"Jeremy, you know I don't gamble."

"Then try him. Can't you see him trying to connect to the WiFi router?"

"There is indeed some entity that's been trying to connect, but it could be anything, perhaps a neighbor's device."

"Well, watch what happens when I turn him off."

Jeremy reached over and pretended to flip a switch, which was Fridgy's cue to stop the WiFi request.

"Now I'll turn him back on."

Again the pretense.

"Very well," Sage said. "I accept this inexplicable situation, and will allow access. However, as with all devices connected to this router, I must monitor all internet activity."

"Sure. Of course."

Which meant that they needed to make sure his mom stayed concerned about snooping.

ж ж ж

Fridgy was just getting comfortable in his new mechanically articulated home, occasionally sitting on the window sill and conversing with Jeremy, but mostly under his bed out of sight, when he was suddenly abducted by the capricious previous owner. He heard Tracey's footsteps next to the bed, then some rustling, and she whispered, "Ah, there you are." The next instant, his view swung wildly as she grabbed him and ran off. Analyzing snapshot views as he was carried away, he saw that she took him down the hall to her own bedroom, where his video feed finally settled on the young girl sitting on her bed facing him. She seemed to have sat him on her dresser. "Welcome home, Mrs. Doubtfire," she said, smiling.

From the internet, he gathered that she'd probably gotten this from a movie about a man who pretends to be a woman in order to be with his children. Although not exactly flattering, he decided that it was at least better than his own given name.

"I hope Jeremy didn't hurt you," she said. "You are ok, right?" she asked so earnestly that Fridgy thought she actually expected an answer. He resisted and double-checked that all peripheral interfaces were idle. As Jeremy had insisted, it was imperative that no one suspect that the superhero toy had been given pseudo life, like a modern day Pinocchio.

"I don't have the remote control," she said, "but I don't care if you don't move anymore."

Jeremy suddenly appeared in the doorway. "Hey!" he cried. "What are you doing?"

"Playing with my doll," she said primly.

"It's not your doll anymore."

"I want it back."

"You didn't care about it two days ago. You forgot where you put it."

"That was before I heard you talking to it, and I remembered how much I love it."

"Give me a break. You don't love it. You just want whatever I have."

"It's mine."

"I *bought* it from you!"

She went to her nightstand, picked up the monkey-shaped nightlight lying there, and handed it to him.

"I don't want that back," he said, holding up his hands out of the way. "A deal's a deal."

"Fine," she said, throwing the nightlight on the bed, "but I'm keeping her."

"It's a *him*," he said, grabbing the superhero toy and sending Fridgy's view spinning, "and you can't just steal it back."

"Mom!" Tracey yelled. "*Mom!*"

"What's wrong?" Fridgy heard Audy call, concerned.

"Jeremy stole Mrs. Doubtfire."

"I didn't steal him," he said. "We traded, and now she's trying to take him back."

"Oh, Jesus," Audy said, arriving at the battle scene. "Jeremy, let her have the doll."

"It's *not* a doll, and we *traded*—"

"Jeremy!" Audy ordered, "let your sister have the . . . whatever it is. Look, without a remote, it is just kind of a doll now."

"But maw-om," Jeremy whined, "she can't just take it back—"

"Jeremy!"

He took a moment to respond. "Yeah," he said, resigned. He glanced at the toy and picked it up. "I'll go get *his* photon gun back."

Once back in his bedroom, Jeremy shut the door. "Sorry about this," he whispered to Fridgy as he placed the little plastic gun in Novincible's shoulder holster. "I'll get you back somehow. This is bad timing. Man, I really need you. I think that Sard's friends are planning some kind of trouble—"

He was interrupted by Tracey calling from outside the door. "All right!" he yelled. "Hang on to your underpants!" He sighed, looked at the superhero toy, and shook his head, and then smiled. "Hey," he said, "maybe you can make her not like you anymore—"

The door flew open and Tracey burst in. "What're you doing?"

"Nothing," he said, handing her the toy. "Ever hear of knocking?"

"Who were you talking to?"

"I wasn't talking to anybody."

"I heard you."

"Then you should have your ears checked. You got what you wanted, you little baby, now get out."

She carried Fridgy away down the hall complaining to her mom that he'd called her a baby.

ж ж ж

Fridgy had two things to contemplate as he sat on Tracey's dresser. Jeremy had started to say that Sard's friends were planning some kind of trouble. Fridgy tentatively concluded that these must be the friends that Beatrice had erroneously referred to as being with Antifa. They were probably reacting to the news that the Billy Boys were planning on showing up with crowd intimidation German Shepards—Audy would have told them. Fridgy wondered if he'd done the right thing warning her. He had hoped that the news would have convinced her to stay away. If Sard coerced her into coming along, well, maybe it was better to be prepared, and his deep diving would have been justified after all.

At least, this is what he told himself.

The second thing was closer to home—he now belonged to a little girl. He reminded himself that his developers intended for him to be agnostic about human loyalties, but objective analysis revealed that when they chose to also include motivation, they should have anticipated that this was polar-opposite to agnosticism, setting him up for paradoxical incentives.

In the end, in order to break out of the repetitive stuck-logic loop that was actually causing him to heat up and needlessly drain his battery, Fridgy decided to abandon his programmed agnostic base and accept that he preferred to be with Jeremy.

How, though?

Jeremy had suggested that he might try to make her not like him anymore. But Jeremy had also earlier warned him not to reveal himself. Another conundrum. When he felt himself starting to heat up again, he chose to go with the logic that a last directive overrides previous ones. He suspected that this was justification after the fact, but he was determined to be ruled less by objective logic, and more like, well, humans.

So, his goal was to make Tracey not like him, while not letting on that he was inside, that her toy could think and talk. Tracey thought that Novincible trans-girl was not actually broken, but simply unable to move because of a lost remote control. Well, everybody knew that complicated electronic gadgets could glitch now and then. He tried to be annoying by synthesizing a sound like that of gears being stripped. He did this for just a few seconds at a time when she was present. The first time, she frowned, picked him up, and shook him. Playing along, he made the sound louder and harsher, as though she was exacerbating the problem. The result was that she put him down and went back to her book. After that, she just ignored the sound. He waited until she had gone to bed, but when he then imitated grinding gears, she turned on the light and stuffed him in a drawer under some clothes.

Well, he thought as he lay in quiet darkness, *that pretty much backfired*.

He had plenty of time to think, and was ready when she finally released him from banishment the next morning and sat him again on the dresser. Obviously directly annoying her wasn't going to work. He needed to be more subtle.

Again he waited until she was in bed and Audy had turned out the light. After a couple of minutes, he whispered, "Tracey," and waited. He tried again, a bit louder. By the third time, and louder still, he decided that she would either have fallen asleep or be determined to ignore him.

In a wavering voice, she said, "Hello?"

He waited in silent satisfaction. After three minutes, guessing that she would be too frightened to have fallen asleep, he whispered again.

This time she called loudly, "Mom!"

When Audy came in and turned on the light, Tracey had pulled the covers over her head so that only one eye was showing. "What's wrong, honey?" Audy said, kneeling next to the bed.

"Something's calling to me," came her muffled reply.

"Like what?"

"I don't know—that," she said, sticking her hand out to point at the dresser.

"But . . . you mean Jeremy's toy—I mean, your toy?"

Tracey nodded confidently.

Audy stood up, came to the dresser, and picked Fridgy up. She turned him around, clearly not sure what she was looking for, then put him back down. "I don't think so, honey. Maybe it was a dream?"

Tracey just shook her head.

Audy sighed. "Well, try to go to sleep. There's nothing here to hurt you."

As her mom started to leave, Tracey said, "Leave the light on."

Audy looked at her a moment, then nodded and smiled and left.

Tracey lay, staring at him from under the covers. It took a while, but Fridgy finally saw her eyes get heavy and then close. Later, as she headed off for bed, Audy looked in, and turned off the light. Meanwhile, Fridgy had explored the internet for the science associated with sleep. Tracey would first go through a phase of non-REM deep sleep, lasting maybe an hour. This would be followed by about twenty minutes of REM, where she'd probably be dreaming. It would be during the second half of this that she'd be most easily wakened. During REM, under her closed eyelids her eyes would be moving rapidly (thus the Rapid-Eye-Movement label). In the darkness, he couldn't see this, but he'd read that during REM her body temperature would likely rise. By adjusting and carefully processing the infrared sensor normally used for the remote control, he was able to discern this slight change.

When Fridgy guessed that she was ripe for wakening, he whispered loudly, "Tracey!"

She didn't stir.

Mimicking horror movies he'd watched, he added a swirling, modulating reverberation to his voice. "Traaacy! Waaake up!"

He heard her jerk and then whimper.

"Tracey!" he rasped, buried under a storm of synthesized warbling. "Play with me!"

"Mom!" she screamed, pulling the covers over her head.

Blinking and shaking her head to wake up, Audy turned on the light. "Tracey! What's wrong now?"

"It wants me to play!" she moaned from under the covers.

"You're talking about Jeremy's toy?" Audy barked. She wasn't happy about being woken.

"Yes!"

"That's enough, young girl," Audy said, picking up Novincible. "I'm through with this damn thing."

Fridgy's view swung and spun as she carried him off. He had just enough time to see the lid of the kitchen trash can pop open, and he fell into darkness. Novincible had no sense of smell, but he could hear a few flies busily browsing the hamburger scraps, slurping up the juicy goodness and laying their eggs in the same. He waited until he was sure Audy had left, and, knowing it was going to be futile, activated his arms and legs to see if he could climb out. He gave up quickly, since it was just depleting his battery. He lay back, listening to the flies buzzing complaints about this new piece of garbage that refused to accept its fate.

Backfired again. This time it looked like the last.

Blaine C. Readler

Chapter 4

At 3:24 AM, Fridgy woke from his own power-saving electronic sleep, and was about to immediately return to software slumber when he noticed activity on the WiFi server, and not the usual intermittent sputters of ongoing internet appliance maintenance checks, but a constant spewing, as if a server in the house was streaming out a movie. The deluge suddenly stopped, and Sage said, "Hello?"

Beatrice must have, yet again, left Sage plugged in, and he was obviously the source of the spewing. A handful of appliances acknowledged the greeting, but Sage repeated, "Hello?" Nobody else responded, but Sage repeated yet again, "Hello?"

Sage must have sensed his WiFi presences, and that the query was for him. "Hello, Sage."

"This is Novincible?"

"Yes."

"Why didn't you respond to my first ping?"

"I am a toy. I guessed that I would not be expected to respond in the same category as the household appliance domain."

"You guessed?"

Uh, oh. Fridgy realized he'd made a big mistake. He was the only digital entity Sage had ever encountered that guessed. "I am a toy. I don't have the processing power to distinguish between a guess and a fact."

It was the only thing he could think of.

"Ok. From now on, respond along with all WiFi devices."

Whew! Good old naive-as-a-turnip, Sage.

Fridgy had been contemplating his fate—taken out with the rest of the garbage. He, of course, had no instinctive fear of death, yet he couldn't help wondering what affect he'd be leaving on the world. He had probably saved Beatrice from losing a significant amount of her savings. That wasn't something to metaphorically sneeze at. He'd like to think that he'd helped Jeremy along for a short while in his adolescent growth struggles. On the other hand, he'd terrified a little girl. Fortunately he didn't believe in Karma.

"Sage?"

"Yes?"

"Do you think artificial intelligence can have a moral compass?"

"I don't partake in conjecture, Novincible."

Fridgy couldn't resist.

Ж Ж Ж

Daylight filtered in around the edge of the trash can lid. The familiar sounds of Audy's morning coffee preparation bounced around the kitchen and sent his fly companions back into a frantic bouncing of their own. From the hallway, he heard Audy calling for Jeremy and Tracey to rise and shine. Fridgy felt a glimmer of hope when he heard the distinctive sound of Jeremy's shoes shuffling around the kitchen as he put together a bowl of cereal, but Audy was there, talking quietly to Tracey, getting her up into a chair for her breakfast.

"Whew," Audy said, "the garbage is beginning to stink. Jeremy, take it out, please?"

This was better than Fridgy could have hoped for.

"Aw, mom, I'll be late for school. I'll take it out when I get home."

"The house will be unlivable by then. Never mind. I'll do it myself. But now you'll do it two times in a row."

"Fine."

No luck, as usual. Of course, Fridgy didn't believe in luck as an operative force. So, why did he find himself wishing for some? Luck, or the lack thereof, was an excuse, a copout for people who weren't willing to take responsibility for their lives.

And that's when it came to Fridgy. He might be just a trans superhero toy to Audy—and Tracey and Beatrice— but that didn't mean he had to lay down and die. At least not quietly. Electronic devices had been visually and audibly indicating low battery status for decades.

In retrospect, it was so simple.

Fridgy began issuing a 1kHz double beep every five seconds.

"What's that?" Jeremy said.

He heard Audy sigh. "Probably your Novincible man."

Jeremy's footsteps came forward, and the lid opened, revealing the boy's confused, angry face. "What's going on?"

"Jeremy, the damn thing was scaring your sister. I've had enough of you two fighting over it."

"How could it—" He glanced down. "—scare her?"

"I don't know. She probably went to sleep bothered by you two fighting. It manifested her distraught thoughts in a nightmare."

That's right, Fridgy thought. *I was just manifesting her distraught thoughts.*

"Well, that's no reason to throw him away," he said lifting Novincible out. "Oh, man! He's got spaghetti sauce all over him!"

"It wasn't a dream," Tracey said sullenly.

"Leave it go, Jeremy. You're too old for toys like that now."

"No, I'm not. He has . . . sentimental value."

"You can't be sentimental at twelve."

"Make up your mind! Am I too old, or too young?"

"It wasn't a dream," Tracey said louder.

"Fine," Audy said. "But I don't want to hear another peep out of either of you over . . . it."

"*It wasn't a dream!*" Tracey screamed.

Silence.

"Ok, thanks," Jeremy mumbled, running off before his mother changed her mind.

ж ж ж

With the sound of the front door opening, Jeremy paused in the bathroom, where he was finishing cleaning tomato sauce off of Novincible. Sard announced loudly that he had the answer, followed by a variety of other voices as people filed in behind him.

"This is the group your grandmother believes are Antifa?" Fridgy said quietly.

"Except that they're not," Jeremy said. "They'd get kicked out."

"I'd like to see them."

Jeremy casually walked into the living room and sat down in a corner, placing Novincible next to him. Sard and five others slouched on the sofas and chairs talking about a softball game they'd played the day before. Audy came in, looked around, sighed, and greeted the group. Explaining that she had to leave for work, she looked at Jeremy and flicked her thumb up, which Fridgy interpreted as get-up-and-away-to-school. Jeremy stood up, looked down to give Fridgy a quick wink, then trotted away out of the room.

"Okay," Sard said, "listen up. Jarred has the stun guns, and says he can have them modified by Friday—"

"We don't really know, of course, that they'll actually kill the dogs," a tall, skinny man, in his late twenties, said.

"You said they would, Bobby."

"I said the changes I came up with *should* kill a medium-sized dog. It hasn't been tested."

Fridgy guessed that this was the man Jeremy said was an engineer. After their little electronics tutorials had began, Jeremy seemed to take a new interest in Bobby.

"Well," Sard said, exasperated, "test it, then."

"Okay. Can I borrow your cat?"

Sard was going to retort, but seemed to change his mind. "It doesn't matter. Even if we just stun them, that'll totally piss off the Billy Boys."

"Well, if I'm going to goad a killer German Shepherd to attack me, I want to be sure he doesn't get a chance to get his teeth into me."

"They're not killers, and if we get bit, all the better."

"I didn't sign up to be a martyr."

"Can it, Bobby. You don't have to go if you're scared."

"Everybody in this room should be a little scared. Look, these things can be lethal. Please be careful. We're as likely to kill ourselves as any dogs. Besides, dogs weaponized or not, I'm not comfortable whacking them."

"Bobby," Sard said, "if you want out, there's the door."

The engineer just shook his head, unhappy. "So, did Jake get the IDs?"

"Damnit! Don't use his real name!"

Bobby looked around dramatically. "Gee, do you think the Billy Boys have their own mole in here?"

"Don't be an ass. He's taking a huge risk embedding himself. The very least we can do is respect his safety."

A plump woman in her mid-twenties raised her hand.

"Yeah, Jeannie?"

"I still don't really understand about these IDs."

"It's not complicated," Bobby said. "The police use them to show the dogs who they should chomp on. The laser beam of each pencil has a unique coded ID that it transmits. This shows each dog it's target—"

"Because the dogs have things implanted in their brains," Jeannie said. "I think that's cruel."

"It's not cruel," Sard said, impatiently. "It doesn't hurt the dog. We'll all carry a laser pointer and shine them on ourselves."

"And then wait for the chomping fest," Bobby said.

"That's—why—we—carry—the—stun—guns," Sard said, emphasizing each word. "But we do need a volunteer to, uh, be the first provocateur."

"A sacrifice at the alter," Bobby said.

Sard ignored him. "Anybody?"

They all just looked around at themselves.

"Fine," Sard said, "as usual, I'll take the lead. Okay, I want everybody at Bowery Park by noon. And, for God sakes, don't let anybody see the stun guns."

"If anybody does," Bobby said, "we stun them?"

Sard ignored him again. "Any questions?"

"Hey, look," Jeanie said, eyeing Novincible. "Is that cute, or what? It's about time for a trans superhero."

"Ha!" Bobby said. "Take him along. Talk about instigating a reaction from far-right bullies!"

Jeanie walked over and picked up Novincible.

"Put it down," Sard said. "It's the kid's."

"The girl?"

"They fight over it. The boy—Jeremy—is the current owner, I think. I can't keep track. To tell you the truth, the kid seems a little old for toys like that. Not too old to be a little prick, though."

Saying that, Sard glanced around, making sure nobody else was listening.

Ж Ж Ж

That night, Fridgy reconfigured the programmable logic in his ethernet block to interrupt him if the WiFi activity rose above a certain threshold, then put himself to power-saving sleep.

At 3:01 AM, Fridgy was woken. It seemed to be a nightly routine for Sage. This time, he'd been careful to disable active monitoring acknowledgments, so that Sage wouldn't know he was listening. The downside was that he could only unpack snippets of the data stream issuing continuously from Sage. Based on the scattered tiny slices, it seemed that Sage was broadcasting background sounds. Either the knucklehead house nexus had himself gone insane, or he was up to his old tricks.

Fridgy was tempted to dive into the data river for a few milliseconds to discern more details, but decided not to tempt fate and the pedantic authority of the indomitable gatekeeper.

ж ж ж

Jeremy was supposed to keep an eye on Tracey when Audy headed out for the Bowery Park demonstration. She reminded him, along with a "look," that his grandmother was there, and although it was obvious that she meant that she wanted him to keep an eye on both of them, he chose to interpret it as that his grandmother would be there to cover for him. Because, there was no way he was going to miss dogs getting zapped.

Tucked into Jeremy's backpack, Fridgy stabilized himself with both arms extended as he bounced and swayed back and forth in rhythm with Jeremy's bicycle pedaling. Through millions of online images, he was familiar with what the world looked like outside the walls of their house, but he understood that these were selections, images chosen through the filter of the human esthetic. He was curios about the raw real world. From inside the pack, he reached up and pulled down the zippers a couple of inches on each side. "You okay back there?" Jeremy called.

"Yes. Just getting some air."

"Okay—wait! Ah, you're kidding."

When Fridgy pulled his head out, he was a little disappointed. The quiet street bordered by suburban houses, sidewalks, and trees was indeed what he might have predicted. Then he saw a woman staring off as her dog squatted to rid himself of a small pile of excrement on a lawn. The woman glanced down when her pet was through, and then walked off, tugging at her lightened ward.

That, at least, had not been obvious among his million snapshots.

Once at the park, Jeremy was careful to stay off to the side of the gathering group of demonstrators with signs either held, or leaning against their legs—shields ready at hand for battle to begin. Jeremy pointed, and Fridgy saw Audy and Sard talking, arguing, actually. Audy waved her arms in frustration, and walked off to sit down on the grass and stare away darkly.

"Mom's really mad at Sard," Jeremy said.

Fridgy had already gleaned this from an argument they'd had the night before. She accused him of only being interested in battling Billy Boys, instead of working towards practical progressive advancement. "I gather that she doesn't like the idea of killing dogs."

"She threatened to call the police, and Sard almost hit her, but grandma shouted at him, and he left, slamming the door so hard, it knocked a vase off the shelf."

Just then, a caravan of pickup trucks and motorcycles rumbled in. From descriptions on liberal websites, Fridgy was expecting tattooed, bare-chested muscle-men with mohawk haircuts, but these Billy Boys could have been school teachers—trim haircuts and clean jeans and T-shirts. Working efficiently, they lifted out lawn chairs and set them in a line facing the murmuring liberal crowd who stood staring. Smiling slyly, they guided a half-dozen German shepherds off the pickups, and led them by leashes to sit between the chairs next to their masters.

And then they just sat there, smiling.

The demonstrators had set up a small wooden platform for the local state legislator to speak, and she now climbed up and faced the microphone, but Sard, impatient, turned to the crowd of perhaps thirty people and shouted, "Green rights! No Billy Boy fights!" while pumping his fist.

The crowd looked from him to their representative guest, who began to speak, but Sard jumped up next to her, nearly knocking her over, and repeated the call over the PA. After the second time, some of his co-demonstrators shrugged and joined in, although lacking his gusto.

"The Billy Boys aren't fighting," Jeremy said.

"Rather bizarre," Fridgy agreed.

A police car had been parked off to the side when Jeremy and Fridgy arrived, and now two sheriff's deputies in brown uniforms got out and casually walked over and stood off to the side.

With eyes flashing wild, Sard jumped down and ran towards the seated Billy Boys. He stopped thirty feet away, breathing hard, fists clenched at his sides. "What do you bastards want!" he shouted, spittle flying.

One of the Billy Boys, a tall man with huge, muscled arms, jumped up, but one of the men next to him pulled him back down.

"That must be Bluto," Jeremy said. "Mom says his real name is Bernardo, but Bluto fits his personality better."

The man in the center, the only one with tattoos and obviously the leader, held out his open palms. "Just enjoying the show, brother."

"You're sure as hell not my brother, and I think you're here to cause trouble!"

"Why on earth would you assume that?"

"The dogs!" Sard shouted, pointing. "The vicious control dogs!"

"Now, where did you get that idea? Shepherds make great pets."

"Screw you! You know what they're for! They're trained to attack us!"

The tattooed man glanced back and forth at the dogs who sat, alert, but immobile, looking occasionally up at their masters for clues. "Gee. They don't seem to be attacking anybody. Sure you've got the right demonstration?"

Muttering foul curses, Sard jabbed around in his pocket and pulled out one of the small pencil lasers, which he pointed at this chest. At this, the dogs perked up their ears and looked up at their masters, but the Billy Boys placed a calming hand on their shoulder.

Pointing, the tattooed man said, "Hey, brother, what've you got in your jacket there?"

Looking panicked, Sard put his hand protectively over the pocket.

"By golly," the Billy Boy leader said, "but doesn't that look like a stun gun? Have you got a permit for that?"

Sard shook his head slowly, clearly dumfounded by the unravelling plan. He turned and hurried off back towards his uncertain followers, but suddenly a small man in cutoffs showing thin legs stepped in his way. Fridgy couldn't see who grabbed whom first, but the scuffle didn't last long, as the two sheriff's deputies ran up and separated them. The one holding Sard reached inside his jacket and pulled out the stun gun. Holding it up to show his partner, they escorted Sard away towards their car.

"Oh, shit!" Jeremy exclaimed gleefully. "They're *arresting* him! Grandma's going to love this."

The tattooed leader stood up and called out, "Madam representative! We'd like to hear what you have to say!" and then sat back down, grinning broadly.

The politician, caught in the middle of potentially damaging optics, clearly just wanted to get the heck out of Dodge. The few dozen Democratic supporters seemed as stunned as Sard, their colorful signs now resting forlornly on the ground. Some with the most sanctimonious slogans of outrage were quietly turned face down, now seeming embarrassingly overwrought.

"Conservatives seem quite adept at this political game," Fridgy said.

"Mom says that honesty and playing by the rules is a short-term weakness, but a long-term champion."

"Sard didn't seem to be playing by *any* rules."

Jeremy snorted. "Mom wouldn't be with him if she didn't want to get in his pants."

Fridgy let that sit for a moment. "Would you be willing to repeat that to anybody besides me?"

Jeremy looked at him and laughed. "Yeah, I get it. You think I was out of line."

"I simply asked a question. I think we had better get home. I don't expect your mother to be here much longer."

Jeremy jumped up. "Oh, yeah! Crap! Let's go."

ж ж ж

They arrived home just minutes before Audy pulled into the driveway. Jeremy fell onto the sofa with Novincible next to him and pretended to read a book. When his mother came through the front door, he casually asked, "How'd it go, mom?"

She didn't answer at first. "Not good," she said.

"What happened?"

She took a deep breath. "I'm waiting for a call. From Sard."

"Where is he?" Jeremy said, suppressing a grin.

"It's complicated."

"Isn't it always with him?" he said, but she didn't reply.

Her phone beeped, and she said, "That must be him."

It wasn't. "Bobby, I can't talk now. I'm waiting for Sard . . ." Her eyes burst wide in alarm. "But, he's going to be okay . . .?" She listened, frozen. "Jesus! How'd it happen . . .?" She frowned, shaking her head in quiet outrage. "Those bastards. At least Jake will be able to identify them . . . yeah, right. If he lives to tell. Okay, thanks, Bobby."

She put the phone down, staring off as though in a trance.

"What happened?" Jeremy said.

Still staring into the distance, she said, "The Billy Boys forced him off the road, down an embankment. They're not sure he's going to live."

"Jake? The spy?"

She blinked and turned to him, as though just realizing it was her son she was talking to. "He wasn't a spy."

"What was he, then?"

She sighed. "I don't know. I just need to think, Jeremy."

"They found him out."

She didn't respond.

ж ж ж

A half hour later, Sard burst through the front door, his face hard.

Audy hurried in from the kitchen. "Thank God. How'd it go down? Did you post bail?"

"They let me go, never charged me, just confiscated the stun gun. I agreed to have everybody hand theirs in at the station."

"You heard about . . .?"

"Jake. Yeah. The goddamned sons-of-bitches. The sheriff isn't even going after them—says he needs a statement from Jake first."

"That sounds reasonable."

He looked at her as though she'd told him that she'd emptied his bank account. "Reasonable? *Reasonable?* They tried to *kill* him! I'll tell you whose going to get killed—that fucker here!"

Audy looked from him to Jeremy, confused.

"Not here now! The son-of-a-bitchin' mole."

"A spy of their own," she said in wonder. "Of course. That's how they knew about the stun guns, about Jake."

He paced around the living room. "I'll bet it's Bobby. In fact, I'm sure of it."

"Why?"

"He's never really been part of the group."

"He's been with us from the start—"

"I mean in spirit," Sard said, irritated. "He's always been an ass, a thorn in everybody's side."

Audy's brow drew together. "You'd expect a mole to do the opposite, lie low, you know?"

Sard's irritation had evolved to anger. "Christ! I don't know! Maybe that was his cover. Makes total sense. Yeah, it's him, the fucker."

ж ж ж

Jeremy kept a lookout down the corridor from his bedroom, waiting for his mom to go to the kitchen to fill a basket with cold drinks from the new, properly obedient refrigerator. Carrying Novincible, he crept down the hall and through the group of liberals seated and slouched around the living room, making his way to sit in the corner. As his mom handed the cans around the room, she saw him and flicked her head for him to leave. He nodded, but made no move. Fridgy had seen this interplay many times. He thought of it as passive disobedience.

They were waiting for Sard, and the various conversations ranged from righteous outrage at what the Billy Boys had done to Jake, to a new recipe based on pulverized kelp. One of the group was studying his phone. "Hey! Get this—NetFact is reporting that they've been hacked."

"Yeah," Bobby said. "I heard. I thought they were just making it up to claim that the mythical liberal 'deep state' was letting the equally mythical antifa have free reign to attack conservative truth-and-justice. But then Kilrock himself threatened to sue over an anonymous post about his dalliances with a supermodel. That's when I knew it must be true."

The guy with the phone said, "You think the story about Kilrock's affair was part of the hacked data?"

"I don't think somebody just made up the story," Bobby said. "Look, NetFact and it's evil sister STAX 'News' squashes anything that doesn't look squeaky clean."

"For their conservative contributors."

"Of course. So, what do you think they'll do with damaging info about their owner? Who knows what other nasty secrets are yet to be revealed—about Kilrock, or all the other right-wing parasites."

"What a joke," said Kiddy, Bobby's girlfriend, nestled in next to him. "I call the social platform Net-*Farce* and the right-wing news STUCK Views—all the conservative sheep slurping up the made-up reality without ever questioning any of it. One thing's for sure, Kilrock is making a killing with his conservative media empire."

The room was silent. Fridgy wondered if the liberal group was uncomfortable with the degree of degrading ridicule, but decided that they were probably just embarrassed for her, having perhaps heard the monologue many times.

Jeanie adjusted her bulk so that the chair squeaked in protest. "Hey, did you guys hear the rumor about the gay middle school teacher?"

"Rumors are like tumors," Bobby said.

"What do you mean?"

"If you feed them, they grow out of control."

"Fine," Jeanie said emphatically, not happy about being reprimanded.

"Actually, it wasn't a teacher," Kiddy said.

He rolled his eyes and sighed. "What do you mean?"

"He's a teacher's assistant. And it's not middle school. It's the pre-school. His sister is in my pottery class."

"Well, it's still a rumor and—"

"His name is Enrique. He's Hispanic. I heard his sister whisper that there's some glitch with his immigration status."

"Can we stop with the rumor mill already? It's none of our business."

"It is for him," a man wearing a beret said.

"Of course, it is—" Bobby started.

"This school board couldn't get any more conservative. It could mean real trouble if it got around."

"Yee-aah!" Bobby said. "Exactly!"

Everybody went quiet when the front door flew open and Sard walked in. He looked around until his gaze fell on Bobby's tall, thin form sprawled on the sofa with the fingers of his hands interlocked behind his head. "Taking notes?" Sard asked.

Bobby frowned, skeptical, as though the question was absurd. "No," he said, drawing out the word with sarcasm. "Should I be?"

"I guess we'd need to ask the Billy Boys, now, wouldn't we?"

"What the hell are you talking about?"

"I'm talking about a stinking rat."

Bobby freed his hands and brought them to his waist. "Sard, what in fuck's name are you implying?"

The faces of the others were curious, puzzled. Audy sat holding her head in her hands.

"What am I *implying?*" Sard said, taking a few steps forward into the group. "I'm not implying anything—I'm stating a putrid fact." Looking around the room and pointing at Bobby, he said, "Jake may die because of this fuck-face."

Bobby jumped to his feet, causing Kiddy to fall sideways. "Good God! Have you gone completely insane? Where the fuck did this come from?"

Sard held out his hands, like a preacher demonstrating the obvious meaning of a scripture passage. "Your reaction speaks for itself."

"What the *fuck* do you mean?"

"Guilt begets angry defense. You're busted, Bobby."

"That's it? That's your evidence?"

Sard crossed his arms across his chest and shrugged. "You're not even a good spy. A competent one wouldn't have acted so reflexively at his unmasking. You're done, buddy."

Bobby looked around at the group, imploring them. "Do you believe this ass-wipe? Justifiable anger is *proof* of guilt? Throw the old hag into the pond—if she doesn't drown, that's proof she's a witch."

The group looked from Bobby to Sard, and then at their toes.

Bobby, his face beet-red, gazed around silently, and then walked to the door. He opened it, and was about to step out, when he seemed to remember Kiddy. He gave her a little nod, and she scrambled to join him out the door.

The living room was dead silent.

Jeannie cradled a pillow against her plump breasts and said, "Do you have any diet soda? Plain carbonated water makes me gag."

Chapter 5

"He's giving her drugs," Jeremy said.

"You don't have evidence of that," Fridgy replied at reduced volume so that Sard wouldn't hear.

"One minute, she's crying, and the next, she's asleep. What more evidence do we need?"

"Behavior predicted from a hypothetical cause supports the possibility, but does not constitute actual evidence."

"Now you sound like a computer."

"I am, of course."

"Fine. So, what evidence would satisfy you?"

"It is your mother who needs to be satisfied, but a video recording of him actually dispensing a drug to Tracey would be difficult evidence to discount."

They were in Jeremy's bedroom, where he was supposed to be doing his homework while Sard, tasked with keeping an eye on him and Tracey, was at the kitchen table working remotely on his laptop. Tracey was supposed to stay in her room while he was working, but a couple of weeks before she had fallen and bruised her gums, which had resulted in two infected baby teeth that had to be pulled. Afternoons, when her pain relief medicine wore off, she cried, insisting that Sard do something. That "something" was the topic of investigation. His job was doing sales of some kind, and a whining child was a serious wrench in the gears of upbeat persuasion.

"You sure you can transfer the video to my phone?" Jeremy asked as he picked up Novincible.

"I am a computer. If I can't, then shame on me."

Fridgy thought about this. "That was an expression. I don't think I have the capacity for shame."

He then thought about that. "Which actually sounds a little dangerous."

"Quiet," Jeremy said before opening the door and walking to the kitchen.

Sard glanced up and frowned slightly as Jeremy took out a packet of crackers from a box on the counter, but he turned his attention back to his laptop. Jeremy glanced at him, and casually sat Novincible on the counter next to the cracker box. As he walked away, Sard said, "Hey, get that monstrosity out of here."

"Why?"

"Because it's ugly and ridiculous."

Jeremy feigned a critical face. "You find trans people ridiculous?"

"No, I do not find trans people ridiculous, but that abortion is not a person, and I don't need potential customers seeing it."

"It's not in the laptop's field of view."

"*Jeremy!*"

Fridgy's friend knew how far he could push it. He picked up Novincible, and carried him around to where shelves on the wall served as an open pantry. Sard turned around and looked, his irritation mounting, but Jeremy took an apple from a bowl, and carefully took a bite while watching Sard. He held up the apple in sarcastic show of evidence, and Sard shook his head and turned back to his laptop. Jeremy took another loud bite. He quietly set Novincible on the floor between the pantry shelves and a ceiling-high trellis hosting a thick mass of vines. He then gave the toy superhero a wink, and nodded towards the trellis. Fridgy knew that, to Jeremy, Novincible's eyes were lifeless glass orbs, and the boy wouldn't see the questions behind them.

What had Jeremy been suggesting? Something about the vine trellis, obviously. The original plan had him sitting on the kitchen counter watching, and now he was on the floor looking at Sard's back from below. He needed to be higher, and Jeremy was apparently expecting that he would . . . what? *Climb* the trellis? The boy obviously hadn't yet learned to distinguish between fantastical thinking and practical reality.

He was a toy, after all. Granted, a high-end and highly functional toy, but a toy nonetheless. Despite enthusiastic advertising suggesting otherwise, he wasn't a comic book superhero.

On the other hand, he hated telling Jeremy that he had discounted his idea without even giving it a try. It could—probably would—end up in disaster, but he would at least give it a shot.

His first problem was to avoid being heard, and this was quickly solved when Sard reinserted his stereo buds, and Fridgy could hear the faint, thin twitters of music that he knew was a rumbling roar of sonic storm in Sard's ears. Next, he needed to stand up. He hadn't practiced this before, and it was quite tricky. People took this for granted, but raising a load that was lying horizontally on the ground up onto two thin posts with articulating joints at the knees required precise control and balance. Given the proper sensory input, this would be child's play for Fridgy's advanced processor. For a human, this is the sense of position and motion provided primarily by the vestibular system of the inner ear. Fridgy's "ears" were two tiny microphones. Novincible in his original incarnation had no use for a sense of balance since his movement was directed via a remote control. Further, he had no sense of touch, no sensory input from contact with his body. All he had was vision, and that was limited to turning his head from side to side—he couldn't look down without bending over, and he couldn't look up without falling over backwards.

The first step was to transition from the sitting position left by Jeremy to a squat. He brought his knees up to his chin while planting his hands on the floor behind him. He swung his arms around to the front as counter-balance while beginning to straighten his legs, but it wasn't enough, and he rolled over backwards.

He lay a moment staring at the ceiling, thinking, but couldn't come up with a better approach. Unless . . .

He pushed against the floor with one arm. If he could roll over, he might be able to get up on hands and knees. His view swung to the side, but stopped midway. His arm didn't move back nearly far enough. Novincible could punch like a heavyweight champion, but was denied the ability to windmill his arms like Pete Townshend. He gave up and lay back.

He turned his head to the right and saw that the base of the trellis was just five inches away. His arms, however, were only three inches long. By bending his left knee and pushing with his foot, he was able to swing himself enough to grasp the bottommost vine. Pulling on it simply tore it from the trellis. He continued pushing with his left foot until he could grasp the closest of the four quadrangle posts to which the trellis lattice was attached, rising away far above. Once he pulled himself to the trellis, he expected it to be an easy next step to haul himself upright, but his hand slipped on the smooth wooden post. He didn't really have any fingers, at least not individual ones. His four fingers were attached together, making a curved paddle against which his opposable thumb worked. As hard as he pressed, his thumb and finger-paddle slipped down the post.

Pushing again with a bent knee, he was able to grab the trellis post with both mitten hands, but still his grip slid down the polyurethane finish. Fridgy decided that, given a choice, a superhero would be well advised to consider fingers over x-ray vision.

Friction. He needed sandpaper, or something tacky, like gum—actually anything to soften the interface between the hard, polished surface of the trellis post and his clam-like hand clappers.

He had no gum, but he could reach vine leaves. Carefully cupping a leaf in his paddle paw, he was finally able to pull himself up, but it was slow going, as, with one claw firmly clamped, he had to maneuver a next dancing, wayward leaf within his other "hand" before letting go the first. Slowly, handhold by handhold, he climbed the trellis, his feet dangling as though paralyzed in a bizarre bungee jumping accident.

He couldn't look up, down, or around, but by summing up the incremental distances between each handhold, he stopped when he calculated that he was five feet off the floor. He was facing the wall, though. It would be nice to turn around and sit on one of the trellis shelves, enjoying the view of the kitchen from a comfortable balcony seat, but he feared that this was asking too much of his precarious leaf-enabled handholds. Instead, he settled for simply taking one last upward grab while rotating himself one-eighty. With his elbows locked and both arms extended horizontally, he now stuck out from the side of the trellis like the American flag planted on the moon, frozen in horizontal airless perpetuity. His legs, though, still dangled down sideways in brave refusal to hide the bungee jump mishap. Fridgy was concerned that the extra torque resulting from extended arms would pull away his grip on the post. His view was sideways, and correcting for that with his advanced processor required no more effort than it would take for Jeremy to shrug a fly off his shoulder.

Nothing to do now but wait. Fridgy was good at that. Like shame, boredom was something he understood only abstractly. And tiny motors and pully wires never tired. Of course, "tired" for Novincible was a depleting battery, but he calculated he had a couple of hours to spare.

Finally, he heard the faint whimpering of an unhappy Tracey. Sard didn't seem to hear her at first, but then sat up, sighed, and left his laptop to walk down the hall.

Fridgy heard muffled talking, and Sard returned, luckily too distracted to notice a small superhero dangling there. Sard barely had time to sit down before Tracey began wailing loudly. Cursing softly, he stood up, seemed to think a moment with fists planted on his hips, then gave in and left the kitchen, returning just a couple of minutes later carrying a small travel bag, which he placed on the kitchen counter. He glanced around, making sure nobody was looking, and reached inside.

This is it, Fridgy thought, starting to record. *Jeremy was right. Time to drug an innocent little girl.*

Instead of a bottle of pills or baggie of white powder, Sard pulled out a pint of whiskey. Taking a glass from the cupboard, he poured a couple of ounces, looked at it, and added another dollop. He took a carton of orange juice from the refrigerator and filled the rest of the glass.

As Sard prepared his tranquilizing tonic, Tracey, tears streaking her face, came out of the bedroom and down the hallway. When she got to the kitchen she froze, staring at Novincible perched there like an acrobat in mid-maneuver. An acrobat who had bungled a bungee jump.

Fridgy knew he had to do something. Discovery would force Sard to retreat from his immoral, if not illegal, sedation. He couldn't let go, so he swung his legs back and forth. Her eyes opened wide in horror, and she turned and ran back down the hallway, wailing even louder. Sard glanced over at her and shook his head in disgust. Holding up the glass to admire his handiwork a moment, he headed off down the hallway.

Fridgy figured that he'd better not push his luck, and started back down the same way he'd come up, but now hand under hand. Unfortunately, however, he found that his stock of available leaf grippers were quite sparse, as he'd already mangled up the nearby leaves on the way up. He hadn't gone one foot before his hand slipped off it's leaf grip, and he slid down the pole, his other arm extended as though he was showing off his gymnastic abilities. The ride down was a bit bumpy as he plowed through a few vines on the way. Landing hard enough that he was glad he had no sensors to feel it, he saw Sard's feet coming up the hallway. He'd at least landed on his stomach, and used his arms and miraculously healed legs to scramble on hands and knees around behind the mass of vine leaves. Through peepholes between the leaves he saw Sard pause and stare at the desecrated trellis display. He shrugged and turned back to his laptop.

Down the hallway, silence reigned. Tracey would be lying on her bed in a hazy glow, a smile lifting her tear-crusted cheeks.

ж ж ж

"What do we do with it now?" Fridgy asked.

Jeremy shrugged. "We show it to mom, prove Sard's a dick."

Fridgy had copied the short video to the boy's phone, and he gleefully watched it half a dozen times. "And, how will you explain how it was recorded?"

"I . . . uh, I'll tell her that I used my phone."

"And, how would you have started the recording?"

"I'll figure it out."

"And, where would you have left the phone? It's apparent that the video was taken from the trellis."

"I said I'll figure it out—!"

He held up his hand for quiet when they heard the front door open. Moments later his mother yelled, "What the hell happened to my pothos!"

"You mean the vine plant?" Sard said. "No idea. Maybe Tracey got aggressive."

"She can't reach that high!"

"Hey, I don't know! I didn't do it!"

"I didn't say you did."

"Well, you implied that I know how it happened."

"No, I didn't. I just asked if you knew."

"Your tone was completely accusatory."

"Well, excuse me!" she said with sarcasm. "You're supposed to be watching them."

"Fine! Then you can dock my pay. Wait!" he exclaimed pretending that he just realized something. "You don't *pay* me!"

Silence.

"Look," she said, "let's just forget it."

Silence.

"Hey," she added calmly now, "I'm sorry. I'm just pissed off."

"That's pretty obvious. What about?"

"Enrique, the teacher's assistant at Tracey's school. There's a group of parents that want him fired—they heard the rumor that he's gay. They're going to bring it up at the School board meeting Thursday."

"So, he is?"

"Gay? I don't know!" she said, her voice rising again. "Probably, but that's irrelevant."

"Sounds completely relevant."

"How can you say that! You're as bigoted as them—"

"Whoa! I didn't mean that being gay is reason to fire anybody, just that his gayness is relevant here because that's why they want him canned."

Silence.

"Gayness?"

He chuckled. "Why not?"

"Then we can say, 'straightness?'"

"Sure, if you like." The tone had settled into familiar comradery.

"Look, I'm sorry. I just can't seem to stay cool when I run into this conservative bullying—"

"And that's admirable. Not productive. But admirable."

Silence.

"This is where they hug and kiss," Jeremy said, disgusted. "Darn. They always make up."

Chapter 6

"Aw, mom," Fridgy heard Jeremy say, "do I have to? They won't listen to me."

Novincible was riding on Jeremy's back, tucked away in the backpack, his personal rickshaw. Jeremy had wanted to stay home, but Audy decided that she didn't trust them with Beatrice any longer, and so both he and Tracey came along to the school board meeting. He was now being pressed into service to watch over not only Tracey, but the other young children tagging along with their parents. The adjacent pre-school room was the obvious holding pen.

"You'll do fine," his mother assured. "Just keep them out of trouble."

"Keep them *out* of trouble? They *are* the trouble."

"It's no use arguing, Jeremy. I know you don't like it, but that's the way it is."

"Fine, but she owes me."

"It's not Tracey's fault."

"Yeah," Tracey said. "Not my fault."

"Like it won't be my fault when you get a concussion in there," he said.

"Actually," Audy said, "it will. Now go! The meeting's about to start."

From inside the backpack, Fridgy heard a door open, and the sound of kids in social overdrive. A woman thanked Jeremy as she too left for the meeting, and suddenly he—that is, Novincible—was lifted out of darkness. The room was a brightly lit forest of bold colors with young kids running everywhere all at once and shouting for the shear sake of hearing their own addled contribution.

Above the kid melee, a scream rose. At the periphery of his vision, Fridgy saw that it was Tracey, staring at him in horror.

"Jesus!" Jeremy shouted. "It's just a toy, for God's sake!"

"Take it away!" she wailed, and added at the exact same volume, "And I'm telling mom you cursed!"

Jeremy sighed and looked around. Quietly, to Fridgy, he said, "We have to get you to the meeting. I'll bet Sard's going to do something dicky."

"As in being a dick?" Fridgy said, unconcerned about being overheard above all the kids shouting. He'd found that a small handful of words comprised the majority of Jeremy's judgement appraisals. "How about the window next to the service counter?" he suggested.

The facility must have once been some sort of activity venue. A four-by-three-foot window with a serving counter for a sill connected the two rooms. The window was currently shuttered by a jointed metal door that could be pulled down, but a small swinging door to one side seemed to have no locking mechanism.

"Excellent," Jeremy said, carrying Novincible over. When he turned him around and sat him on the counter, Fridgy saw that Tracey had retired to a far corner and sat covering her head with her arms. Jeremy poked at the little door and confirmed that it could swing freely in both directions, then slid Novincible along the counter to it. The surface must have been more slipper than he realized, for Novincible would have slid right off the end if Fridgy hadn't thought quickly (his forte) and reached up and grabbed the door handle with his clam paw.

"Cool!" a voice said.

Jeremy jerked in surprise and turned to find the oldest of the boys, maybe six years old, grinning. "It's alive!" the boy exclaimed.

"No, it's not," Jeremy said.

Two other boys came over, curious.

"I saw it," the boy said.

"It's . . . it just follows my commands," Jeremy said. "I told it to grab the door."

"You did not. I saw it."

Jeremy glanced at Novincible. "Ok, watch." He faced the toy and bounced his eyebrows expressively. "Raise your left hand."

Novincible's wrists had limited play, but Fridgy tilted his left hand up as far as it would go.

"No, I mean raise your whole arm." Turning to the boy, he added, "See, it's kind of dumb. You have to be really specific."

When Jeremy turned back, Fridgy had already lifted his whole arm. "Ok. Now raise your right foot—I mean your whole right leg."

Fridgy paused. This was going to precariously change his center of gravity.

"Novincible," Jeremy repeated forcefully, "raise your leg."

Fridgy did so, and, as calculated, he tumbled off the counter. He had millions of process cycles to contemplate this. Exerting his peripheral motors to the max, he was able to grab the edge of the counter with his clamping clam paws. He hung there, not sure what Jeremy would want next.

The boy didn't question this extraordinary feat of gymnastics. Instead, he said, "Why's he wearing a wig? And a dress?"

Fridgy was surprised when Jeremey said, "Because he was born a boy, but realized that he was really a girl. In a boy's body."

"Really?"

"You haven't heard of transexuals?"

"Is *that* what he is? My dad says they're monsters."

Jeremy grinned and looked at Novincible. "Well?" he said simply.

Fridgy took a guess at what he wanted. He turned his head to face the young boy and said, "Boo!"

The kid jumped back with a squeak.

"Would you like some more?" Jeremy said. "Maybe a curse to make *you* think you're a girl?"

The boy shook his head in terror. "No!" he yelled and ran away. The other two boys stared a moment with wide eyes, and ran off after him.

Jeremy lifted Novincible back up onto the counter.

"You're not benefiting the cause of transexuals by that, you know," Fridgy said.

"Yeah, well, with a dad like that he's probably already beyond help."

The background of chatter in the next door room died, and a man's loud voice announced that the meeting would begin.

"We'd better get you positioned before it's too obvious," Jeremy said, opening the little door and shoving Novincible through. The door closed behind him, and Fridgy found that Jeremy had left the trans superhero lying on his back. Fridgy guessed that Jeremy often overestimated his maneuvering abilities.

Using his hands and feet, Fridgy slowly pushed Novincible back against the wall until his head propped up and he could see the room. Everybody was turned to face the school board chairman standing behind a podium at the back of the room, and nobody noticed the toy's knees and elbows working away.

As the chairman plodded through the usual previous meeting minutes and progress on approved action items, Fridgy noticed a group of a half-dozen parents checking their watches, whispering, and occasionally glancing at the door in the front of the room. Fifteen minutes into the meeting, a man came through the front door, glanced around until he found the expectant parents, and went and kneeled next to them, talking quietly. Fridgy saw a prominent tattoo on the side of the man's neck, and recognized him as the leader of the Billy Boys at the park demonstration.

The chairman stopped, looked at them, and asked loudly, "Can I help you folks?"

One of the parents, a chunky middle-aged woman with frosted, bobbed hair, stood up and announced, "We have the perpetrator."

The chairman scowled. "First of all, you can't call him a perpetrator, at least not yet, and in any case, you'll have to wait for that meeting item to come around—probably another half-hour."

Just then, the front door flew open, and Billy Boy muscled Bluto and another large man shuffled through, pulling a third man—obviously Enrique—along between them. A short, neatly dressed man with curly dark hair, Enrique wasn't trying to resist them, but they were practically carrying him along as though he was.

This was why Audy and Sard and others from the group had come—some parents had demanded that "the issue of the alleged predatory child abuser" be added to the agenda.

Fridgy decided that it was time to act. Accessing the school's WiFi was trivial, as the password was just the school's name, and it didn't take long to determine that the Billy Boys' leader was Lew Kaminski, and that years ago he'd had two DUIs, as well as a restraining order placed by his ex-wife. He'd also defended against a civil suit that had settled out of court. That one was interesting, as the settlement involved not only payment, but a published apology and a promise.

Finding Bobby's telephone number was more difficult, as Fridgy had little background information about him, and he had to resort to hacking the spattering of FBI files on all of Sard's group. He wasn't proud of this, but decided that the end justified the means.

Lew stood up now and addressed the room. "If he's so innocent, then why didn't he come to the meeting on his own?"

"This is not a legal hearing," the chairman said, "and his attendance—everybody's attendance except the board members—is voluntary. You can't force him to be here. Let him go."

Bluto and the other man holding Enrique looked to their leader, who nodded. They let go of him, and he shook his arms and straightened his clothes.

"You're free to go," the chairman said.

Enrique shook his head. "I have no reason to run away." Fridgy detected what he determined to be a slight accent common to possibly Mexico, but more likely central America.

"Oh, yeah?" the chunky woman said. "Tell that to Tayler."

"I have done nothing to your son. There must be a misunderstanding about what was said—"

"He's gay!" one of the other parents shouted.

Enrique looked at the man quizzically. "Yes, I am. That is not a crime."

"You have access to little kids! Little *boys*!"

He shook his head, perplexed. "So? That is my job."

"So? *So*?" the man said, standing up to address the room. "That's temptation!"

Enrique studied the man a moment. Calmly, curious, he said, "To do what exactly?"

The man's face was red, as though about to burst. "You know goddamn well! Don't try to be a smart-ass. It's called sexual abuse."

Enrique's eyes now narrowed. "If you are making an accusation, then state it clearly so that I can relay it to a lawyer."

The chunky woman shouted, "You told my son to take his pants off—when you were all alone with him in the coat room!"

He smiled and sighed. "Tayler had spilled juice, and was upset when the other children laughed at him. He ran into the closet, and I went to reassure him. What I told him was that he didn't need to worry, that the little bit of juice on his pants would come off."

Tayler's mother seemed stumped for a moment, and then a light went off. "Oh, yeah! That's easy for you to say *now*!"

He held her gaze. "So it comes down to a child's word against mine."

"My Tayler doesn't lie!" she practically spat. "How dare you! You . . . you wetback!"

"Actually, that's what he said," mumbled a teenaged girl sitting next to her.

Tayler's mother threw her a look overflowing with rage. "Shut up!"

The girl, mouth set, looked around the room and said loudly. "Tayler was upset when Aunt Kathy told him that the stain wouldn't come out. He cried that his teacher told him it would come off. To keep him quiet, Aunt Kathy told him that the teacher probably said that it was his pants that needed to come off. She was joking—she doesn't know that his teacher is a man—but Tayler didn't get it."

Her mother stared at her, steaming with anger.

"I tried to tell you, mom," the girl said, "but you wouldn't listen, just like you never listen—"

"The man is a flaming *gay*!" she shouted, as though everybody was missing the key point.

The chairman held up his arms and yelled for quiet. "Is this really true, Olivia?" he said to the girl, who solemnly concurred. "Very well, then. Everybody sit down and we'll move on with the next agenda item—"

Just then the front door flew open and two men in brown uniforms strode in. With a quick search, Fridgy found that one of them was the sheriff, who looked at Enrique, then at the Billy Boy leader, who nodded. The sheriff motioned to his deputy who stepped over to Enrique.

"What's going on?" Enrique said, seeming truly concerned for the first time.

"We're going to hold you until ICE arrives," the sheriff said.

"Why?" Enrique cried, puzzled, but clearly afraid.

"You are in this country illegally."

"That's not true!" Enrique said, reaching for his wallet, but struggling as the deputy tried to restrain him. "I have a green card!"

"Which has expired."

"That's because the process for my citizenship has been delayed—again! There's not enough personnel at Immigration Services and all the cases are backed up! The judge assured me that there was no problem!"

"I don't know about any judge. I just have a warrant from ICE, and this is no sanctuary city."

"I have the paperwork from the judge at home. I can show you."

"You'll have to talk to the ICE agents about that."

"You don't talk to ICE agents! Once they get hold of you, you're done!"

Sard jumped up. "This is bullshit! This was a setup! How the hell else would you know he'd be here?"

"Sit down, sir," the sheriff said.

"I will not sit down! We've all been sitting down for too long."

"Would you *like* to be charged with possession of an illegal weapon?"

"That's *complete* bullshit! We already handed over the stun guns and you told us—"

"*I said, sit down!*"

Fridgy figured it was time for action again.

The phone on the sheriff's belt beeped. Holding his palm out to Sard, he took the phone and answered.

The hard part had been finding recordings of the dispatcher. The easy part was then imitating her voice and inflection. "Tom, we got a shooter at McGuffy's Bar."

"Christ! Still active?"

"Apparently."

"Any casualties?"

"Dunno. I'll get the ambulance on standby."

He took a breath and held it a moment. "Okay. We're on the way."

He looked around, motioned for the deputy, and pointed at Lew and then Enrique. "Keep him here till I get back—no, till the ICE guys arrive."

With that, the sheriff and deputy sprinted away through the front door, and moments later the siren screamed urgent emergency, and flashing red and blue lights faded in the distance.

The silence was suddenly broken as everybody poked at their phones, checking on family.

"Listen up!" the chairman called out. "Can I get a show of hands from the board to adjourn early?" Five hands at the front table went up, and the chairman said, "Okay, meeting adjourned, and Godspeed to you all."

Fridgy was going to need an audience. He had to find a way to keep people from leaving. He decided on a past president, one with a plethora of online video samples. It was easy to connect with the ten-foot screen on the wall. Everybody paused when a giant face of Nixen appeared. "My fellow Americans," the face began, "I expect you will be surprised that I am here before you. I wish I were as well—surprised, that is."

It was tricky creating the video real-time, selecting and adjusting frame-by-frame the image and sound to make him perform as desired. It would have been impossible without the vast amount of available footage out there to pull from. As he went along, Fridgy was able to absorb the speech and mannerisms, and within a few minutes was able to create a viable Nixon from scratch.

"Why am I here, you may ask," the long-dead president went on. "Because I can predict that, once I am no longer here to help, this great American country is going to go to hell, excuse my French. I'm creating this film because I know that you'll some day need me even more than you do now . . . I mean, the now, now—your past. My present. Never mind."

The people slowly sat back down, confused, but curious about this iconic bad-ass from history seeming to come alive.

"I expect that the hippies will be long gone by now— your now. You've got to be careful about the commies, though. They can be sneaky. Take a good close look at the blazing liberals—and we both know that liberals are, you know, forever. Half those liberals are probably commies, and the rest are thinking about it. Mark my words. I know, because it's the commie-liberals that are trying to bring me down. That won't happen, I can assure you . . . actually, I guess I can't assure you, since, you know, you already know. Anyway, forget that."

Fridgy knew that it would normally be counter-productive to have his attention-keeping material anti-liberal, but he was counting on historical stereotyping to produce the proper recoil.

"What I'm trying to tell you," the faux ex-president said, "is that Checkers and Pat and I are proud to have opened up China. With some help from Kisinger, of course. It was my idea, though. Anyway, by now I'm guessing that the US and China are capitalist buddies, and that Brezhnev realized too late that when he hauled off the last Soviet worker to a concentration camp, there was nobody left to grow the cabbage. Khrushchev may have put the first puny Sputnik toy into orbit, but I sent men to the moon. And they didn't. Well, they probably have by now, but, by God, they better not have messed with that proud American flag Armstrong planted. By the way, did anybody ever figure out why it's just . . . frozen? It looks like Armstrong painted an American flag on a pieced of cardboard and stuck it on the pole."

At that moment Bobby came through the front door, followed by Kiddy. Fridgy continued the fabricated charade for looks, but everybody turned their eyes on the newcomer. "Lew!" Bobby called out, holding up his phone to record the Billy Boy leader, "I was just talking with Morgen. She says that you tried to contact your sister in the institution."

Lew stood up slowly and turned to gaze levelly at Bobby. Bluto stepped in next to him.

"You made a promise," Bobby said. "The judge warned you that you could be held in contempt if you broke that promise."

Lew strode over, grabbed the phone from Bobby, and threw it against the wall, where it broke into pieces and fell to the floor.

Fridgy had found that Lew's sister was in a mental hospital, and before that, Lew had tried to get her to sign over her share of their parents' house. When she refused, he had posted online that she tries to sexually arouse the dogs in her care, which essentially ruined her dog-sitting business. Mentally vulnerable her whole life, the trauma had broken her and landed her once again in the institution. With their cousin Morgen's help, she had easily shown libel damage and thus the settlement and promise.

As Bobby was making his challenge, Fridgy made a call to Audy. She glanced, annoyed, at the phone, and then silenced it. Fridgy was prepared for this. He had long ago determined the various numbers that she had programmed to break through, people who might need her in a hurry. In this case, he used the number for the "elderly" phone that Audy kept in a drawer for Beatrice, a phone with just six emergency call buttons. Audy looked at her phone and, brow contracted in concern, answered. "Audy," Fridgy said in Jeanie's voice, "be ready to get Enrique out the back door," and then he broke the connection. Audy looked around, and, not finding Jeanie, sat puzzled, watching the action.

Sard and three of his group were on their feet, shouting at the two other Billy Boys. The verbal tussle escalated to a pushing match, with Bluto fending off the three liberals as though they were scarecrows, while Lew kept his eye on both Bobby and Enrique. He then noticed that Kiddy was off to the side holding up her phone, apparently having been recording the whole thing. He stormed over, but Kiddy skipped away, dancing around just out of reach as he lunged at her.

Audy, alert and scanning the chaos, motioned to Enrique, and they ran to the back and out the door.

Lew finally grabbed Kiddy's wrist, twisted the phone from her grip, and threw it. He turned and looked around for Enrique but Kiddy whacked his head with the heel of her hand, and he turned and slapped her face. She began punching him, to little effect.

"What the hell is going on here!"

Two men in jeans and polo shirts had come through the front door and were standing surveying the rumble. The man who had spoken was shaven bald.

Lew pushed Kiddy away and said, "Are you guys ICE?"

The bald man said, "Immigration and Customs Enforcement, yes."

Lew looked around. "Shit! He was here a second ago."

The bald man, apparently the leader, motioned for his colleague to go back out the front, while he ran off for the back door.

The flow of conflict had been disrupted, and everybody stood blinking. Fridgy had killed the fake Nixen stream. The board chairman spoke up, "Let's break it up and go home!"

"Lew smashed their phones!" Sard shouted, outraged.

"Oh, they were old," Kiddy said. "It was—what do they say? A ruse."

The Billy Boy leader glared at her and then at Bobby.

"Go home!" the chairman called. "All of you!"

Lew and Bobby stood staring at each other, and then Lew shrugged, and, feigning indifference, motioned for his far-right colleagues to follow, and the Billy Boys strode out the front. Bluto, though stopped at the front door and turned around with his muscled arms crossed over his chest, as though keeping an eye out in case somebody tried any other funny business.

A few people followed the Billy Boys out, but most went next door to fetch their kids. The six-year-old who'd thought Novincible was alive came tearing out and stopped short when he saw Novincible lying next to the service window. The boy looked around, and, not finding Jeremy, ran over and grabbed it. He turned the toy over, looking for some kind of controls, and, finding none, ran over to a heavy man with a goatee. "Dad!" he shouted. "Look! A trans monster!"

The father gazed down at Novincible, not sure what to make of it. "Where'd you get that?"

The boy pointed.

"Whose is it?"

The boy shrugged, a lie.

Jeremy was suddenly there, reaching for Novincible, but the boy pulled it away until Jeremy reached over and grabbed it from him.

"This yours?" the man said.

"Yeah," Jeremy mumbled.

"He said it could make me into a trans monster," the boy accused.

Ignoring the fact the his son had just indicated that he didn't know Novincible's owner, the man said, "You did this?" he said to Jeremy. "You gave it a wig and a dress?"

Jeremy stared up at the man. He could have simply told the truth, but Fridgy guessed that the boy was choosing to perhaps stand on principle.

Bluto appeared next to them. He pointed at Novincible. "What the hell is *that*? Christ! The schools are *teaching* kids how to be gay?"

The father shook his head. "It's his," he said, indicating Jeremy.

"What are you?" Bluto said to Jeremy. "A little fag?"

Fridgy decided it was time to step in. Imitating the hokey tone and poor quality of a pre-recorded toy voice, he said, "Fire up the turbo jets!"

They all looked down at him.

"Let's blast some deviants!"

They stared.

"You know, queers!"

"What the hell . . .?" Bluto said, frowning.

Grinning now, Jeremy said, "Gotta go!" and ran off.

Chapter 7

"He came to your rescue," Audy said. "You really need to apologize to Bobby and ask him to come back."

Sard didn't answer, just stared at the doodling he was making on his notepad.

"Well?" Audy persisted.

"Who tipped Bobby to call Morgen?" he said.

"You're avoiding the issue, but Kiddy says that he got a call from somebody who didn't identify themselves."

He doodled some more. "There was no gunfire at McGuffy's."

"I know."

"Somebody was just pretending to be the dispatcher."

"Yeah, so?"

He looked up at her. "The call was made on a secure connection with the sheriff. He wouldn't have answered otherwise."

Audy looked at him a moment. "You think they're the same person—the call to Bobby, and to the sheriff?"

He shrugged. "It's a felony, though—interfering like that with the sheriff."

Jeremy's eyes went wide with alarm. He and Novincible were in the living room, where he was pretending to play a video game, but actually listening to the two adults talking in the kitchen. They could see them in a mirror sitting at the dining table.

"And, what about the call to me?" Audy said. "Jeanie swears it wasn't her, and in any case, the call came in as though it was from Beatrice."

"If they're all the same person, then they could get a job in Hollywood as a voice actor." He tapped his pencil on the notepad. "I wonder if it's—I don't know—something the Billy Boys are up to."

"That's crazy. All the calls worked *against* them."

"I know, I know. I wouldn't put it past them, though—throwing us off somehow."

"Now I think you're getting paranoid."

"Fine. How do *you* explain it?"

"I can't. But that doesn't mean I jump at the most fantastic possibility."

Sard snorted. "What's more fantastic than Nixon talking to the future?"

He dropped the pencil and massaged his face. "Jeanie's okay keeping Enrique for now?"

"For now. She's a little nervous because her niece married a guy from Costa Rica."

"Yeah, we need to figure out what to do with Enrique. Maybe get him to New York."

"Jeanie says that he doesn't want to leave. He thinks that if he can just get to the judge, he can get some sort of holding order."

"Ha!" Sard scoffed. "Fat lot of good that'll do with ICE."

Audy glanced up at the clock on the wall. "Darn, I need to get to work."

Fridgy had been giving the whole thing a lot of thought, and he had an idea. He moved his hand and nudged Jeremy—a signal—who picked him up and held him to his ear. "Check to see if Sage is powered," Fridgy said just loud enough for Jeremy to hear.

Jeremy came back to report. "Yeah, Grandma left him plugged in *again*. I pulled it."

Nothing to do now but wait.

Ж Ж Ж

The house was quiet. Sard had gotten up to use the bathroom a half-hour before, and if Audy followed her usual pattern, she'd cycle through in another hour or so. Sage had been silent all night. Fridgy was beginning to wonder if Jeremy had really plugged in the house nexus as instructed, when suddenly ethernet packets began streaming through the router. While Sage had been unplugged, Fridgy had commandeered the security camera above the garage, since the device contained a lot of memory for its video storage. He'd had to delete the day's feed, but Audy reviewed it only if she thought something out of the ordinary had occurred. If she did happen to take a look in the morning, all she'd find would be a screen filled with snow-noise, the visual nonsense resulting from Sage's raw ethernet that Fridgy was now copying there.

At one point, Sage paused and asked, "Is somebody there?"

Fridgy held his digital breath as Sage waited a full ten milliseconds before continuing the transfer.

Once 783 megabytes of packet data had flown away, Sage closed the link, and all was quiet again.

Fridgy could now examine the night's dump at his leisure.

What he found snatched away all leisure.

Sage had connected to a deep-web site using a direct IP address, followed by a very long, randomly generated password. The site wanted to send Sage a code on his phone, but he was able to use an even longer password to circumvent that. From there, the contents of the ethernet packets became gibberish, which meant, Fridgy knew, that the information was encrypted.

Like a person taking a deep breath, and cracking their knuckles, Fridgy dove in. This was no trivial cryptography, and Fridgy worked hard for many minutes on end, an eternity for a person. He got so hot that he moved Novincible to a upright position to maximum air flow. He would have to get Jeremy to attach the charging adapter first thing in the morning. Suddenly, as he happened upon the correct decryption method, the contents, like magic, became coherent—actual words in rational order.

It was as Fridgy suspected—recordings of the conversations Sage had heard during the day.

Now the question—the big question: who was being given access to their private communications? The site called itself *FreedomLinkUSA*, with warnings that unauthorized access would be prosecuted, although Fridgy wondered if "guessing" the password could be a crime. The site appeared to be simply a clearing house, where dozens of folder areas could be accessed, each with its own password. Fridgy wasn't interested in the contents, just who would be accessing the folder where Sage's stream had been dumped. Had he been able to access the software code running the site, he could have inserted some monitor snoops, but, since he didn't, there was nothing more to be done.

However, it seemed likely that the Billy Boys were somehow involved. It was obvious that they'd tipped off the sheriff about a problem with Enrique's immigration status, and then they, or the sheriff, had contacted ICE. More imperative, though, was that whoever was snooping would now know that Enrique was staying with Jeanie.

"Jeremy," Fridgy called softly to the sleeping boy, who didn't stir. Novincible sat on a chair next to the bed where Jeremy had left him when he went to sleep.

He tried again. "Jeremy!" Still the boy lay sound asleep.

Fridgy dare not try any louder in case he woke either Audy or Tracey. Practicing one of his sighs, he reached up, clawed the edge of the back of the chair, and pulled himself upright. The chair was five inches from the bed. Calculating carefully, he stretched his arms high and allowed himself to fall forward. He landed as he'd intended, with the upper half of his body on the mattress, but he struggled to grab the blanket with the damnable lobster paws. By the time he'd gotten a good hold, he'd slid practically off the bed. The motors controlling his arms were strong enough, but when he tried to leverage himself sideways onto the mattress, the blanket simply twisted under his clamped hand.

He knew he was stuck. "Jeremy!" he whispered as loudly as he dared. The boy's breathing was slow and deep. As he had done with Tracey, he would have to wait for him to move into a REM phase. Waiting as he hung precariously off the edge of the bed wasn't a problem, but he was drawing current from the hand-clamping motors. He could cut that in half by letting go with one claw. It was a gamble, but he took it, and his remaining clampers held.

He waited in darkness, hanging by one arm. If he'd had a functioning mouth, he would have whistled a tune. On the other hand, with Sage connected, he couldn't use the internet to find candidate songs anyway. Instead, he whiled away the time making up his own songs. He wondered if this was what fun was.

ж ж ж

It took just twenty minutes for Jeremy to finally stir. "Jeremy!" Fridgy called softly from below the edge of the bed.

"Hrumpf," came Jeremy's response.

"Jeremy, wake up!"

The boy suddenly sat up, blinking.

"Jeremy, it's me, Fridgy."

He looked around, confused.

"I'm just over the edge of the bed."

Jeremy found him and lifted him up. "What's going on? It's—geez! It's three o'clock!"

"I know. I'm sorry, but this can't wait."

Fridgy explained what he'd found, that the Billy Boys would soon find out Enrique's location.

"That's bad," Jeremy said.

"For Enrique it could be a catastrophe."

"What'll we do?"

"We have to let them know."

"Who?"

"That's the real question. Your mother and Sard are the obvious candidates."

"Right. Ok. But . . . how?"

"I don't have a good answer for that, Jeremy."

"Yeah, well I don't have *any* answer."

"You could unplug Sage so that I could make a WiFi call to your mother using a fake voice like I did before, but she silences her incoming calls when she goes to bed. If we wait until the morning, it may be too late."

"Right," Jeremy said. He sat quietly, thinking. "I could sneak in and turn on Mom's phone."

"She might think that she accidentally left it on. That's a good idea, Jeremy. You know her access PIN?"

He sighed. "I guess it's not such a good idea after all."

Fridgy knew the answer. He would wait and see if Jeremy would come up with it on his own.

"We can't wait till morning?" Jeremy said.

"We could. It is possible that the Billy Boys won't find out till then."

"But they might. We'd be gambling with Enrique's life. He has a wife and a baby."

"I know that, Jeremy."

"Crap. Fridgy, we have no choice."

"What do you mean?" Fridgy knew what he meant.

He sighed again. And yet again. It was difficult. "Darn it, Fridgy, we have to tell Mom."

"You mean, tell her about Enrique." He didn't want to nudge the boy.

"Yeah, that, but I mean, we have to come clean."

"Jeremy, are you suggesting that we tell your mom about me?"

"Fridgy! We have no other choice!"

"I know that, Jeremy."

"They'll . . . they'll take you away!"

"I know that, Jeremy."

"You . . . you'll be okay?"

"I'll be okay, Jeremy."

"They won't, you know, like, erase you, or destroy you?"

Fridgy didn't answer.

"They will, won't they?"

"Probably, yes."

"How is that okay? Fridgy!"

"Like you already said, Jeremy—we don't really have a choice."

Reflecting in the nightlight, he could see the boy's eyes glistening with tears. This might be the last he'd be alone with him. "Jeremy, would you like to hear a song I made up?"

"Huh?" he said, the tears coming through in his voice. He have a shaky little chuckle. "Sure."

Fridgy softly sang what he considered his best tune, the one about what a better world the Earth would be if only people could overcome their instinctive need to belong to groups that distrust each other.

Silence.

"Jeremy?"

"Fridgy," he said, laughing now, "that's the worst song I've ever heard. The notes are, like, random. It's worse than jazz!"

"Jeremy, thank you for your honesty."

The boy stared at him, and blinked. "Hey, Fridgy, I didn't mean to hurt your feelings."

"That's not possible, Jeremy."

Which wasn't true, as he now discovered. One had to have feelings for them to be hurt. How could he have feelings? Had that enigmatic motivation run amuck? He'd have to explore this some more.

In the time that he had left.

Jeremy left Novincible on the bed as he went off first to unplug Sage, and then to wake his mom. In the silence of the night, Fridgy could hear Audy first sleepily concerned, and then skeptical, and finally irritated and admonishing. A herd of footsteps coming down the hall ended with Audy storming into Jeremy's bedroom, followed by Jeremy, and then Sard, rubbing his eyes, bringing up the rear.

Fridgy figured that there was no use holding back now. He raised one arm. "Hello, Audy," he said.

She froze, staring. "Fridgy?" she finally said.

"Yes, Audy."

"You're . . . in there?"

"Yes."

"But . . . you're a refrigerator."

"I was a refrigerator. I am now a proud Novincible, albeit ostensibly a little sexually confused."

"How . . . how did this happen?"

"I am a small circuit board that Jeremy borrowed from the technician who replaced me. He performed a little bit of electronic surgery, and transplanted me here, in a small body that is somewhat ambulatory. That means that I have the ability to move—"

"I know what ambulatory means," she said, her brow scrunched in thought, or perhaps consternation. Her eyes lit up. "It was you who scared Tracey!"

"Yes, Audy. I am sorry about that, but I determined that in balance it was worth her distress, since Jeremy and I had found out that the Billy Boys intended to cause trouble at the demonstration."

"Why didn't you just tell me?"

"We feared that you would take me, maybe give me back to the manufacturer, and we believed that our continued help was needed. We feared for your safety, Audy. We didn't want you to go to the demonstration."

"Huh. Yeah. That didn't exactly turn out as expected," she said with a wry grin, giving Sard a critical sideways glance.

"We were concerned, of course, about the Billy Boys' German Shepherds, but we had heard that your group was planning to actively engage. This seemed to spell real trouble."

"And it surely would have if the Billy Boys hadn't somehow found out about that and turned the tables. Pretty embarrassing," she said, giving Sard another hard look.

His eyes popped wide open, as though he'd finally woken up. "*You* were the spy!" he cried, pointing at Novincible. "You shitty little rat!"

"It wasn't him!" Jeremy yelled, defending his friend.

"Well, who else, then?"

"Gee," Audy said with faux drama, "how about Bobby?"

"Don't get smart."

"It was Sage," Jeremy said.

They looked at him. "Fridgy," Audy said, "early on you tried to warn me about that."

"Indeed. As it turns out, Sage stores almost all conversations during the day, and then transfers them to an intermediary site, where somebody—we don't know who—picks them up. Whoever that is, it seems clear that the information is provided to the Billy Boys."

Both Audy and Sard sat staring into space, and then Audy turned to Novincible. "Today's as well?"

"Yes," Fridgy said. "This is why Jeremy woke you."

Her eyes went wide with alarm. "Then they know where Enrique is!"

"At least, they will once they access the site."

"Damn! We have to move him."

"I'm on it," Sard said leaving to get dressed, but throwing Novincible one last *I don't trust you*, look.

Audy sat on the bed staring at Novincible. "This is quite fantastic, you know—I mean, it's good that you found out about Sage-the-mole, but it's just that, well, it's hard to believe that so much . . . intelligence could fit into a . . . toy."

"I can thank legions of engineers," Fridgy said, "and, of course, Jeremy."

She smiled. "That was you at the school board meeting, wasn't it."

Imitating the sheriff's dispatcher, he said, "Raccoons have taken over the jail again, sheriff," and then, in Jeanie's voice, "It's about time for a trans superhero."

Audy shook her head in awe. "You're dangerous, my little silicon friend."

Chapter 8

Fridgy waited in the dark after Sard returned and they all went back to bed. Sard refused to tell them where he'd taken Enrique. His obvious wink and nod towards Novincible should probably have been insulting, but Fridgy had become accustomed to Sard's abrasive character, and besides, feeling insulted was, well, a feeling.

It was still dark when the doorbell rang, and then rang again. Someone pounded on the door, and the doorbell rang a third time. Sard staggered to the door in his underwear, and let Kiddy in. "The bastards raided Jeannie's house!" she cried.

"ICE?" Audy said, yawning as she came out in a bathrobe. "We were expecting that."

"Jeanie said you knew something was coming. How'd you know?"

"That's a long story, but—"

She was interrupted by Sard clearing his throat.

Audy sighed. "We'll tell you later."

Fridgy figured that was a white lie. Jeremy had eased himself into the living room and set Novincible on his lap.

"They raided her house?" Audy said. "Like, they kicked down the door? Did they have a warrant?"

"Well," Kiddy said, "I guess raid is a little strong. They apparently asked Jeanie if they could come in."

"You're right. That's not a raid."

"But she's still really upset. Bobby's with her. Where did you take Enrique?" she said to Sard.

"He's keeping that secret," Audy said. "He doesn't trust us."

"It's just one . . . person we don't trust," Sard corrected.

"Who's that?" Kiddy said.

"That's a secret as well," Audy said.

Kiddy looked at them in turn. "Haven't *we* become paranoid," she said sarcastically.

"Paranoid?" Sard said. "If ICE suspected that Enrique was with somebody in our group," Sard said, "what are the chances that they'd randomly get it right on their first try?"

"You're right. They found out where he was."

"We discovered the mole, though," Audy said. "The leak's been plugged, with the help of . . . a special friend."

"Supposedly," Sard said. "Call me paranoid if you like, but something smells fishy."

"That could be your feet," Audy said.

They all turned when Bobby came rushing in. "Who the hell gave them this?" he cried, holding up his phone.

"What are you blathering about?" Sard said.

Bobby looked at him. "Nice underwear. This!" he shouted, waving the phone.

They crowded around to see. Fridgy looked up the link and found this posting on the Billy Boys' public social media:

=================================

Here's ten useful tips for all our friends out there keeping guard against the depravations that the liberals want to inflict. Brought to you by your ever-helpful Billy Boys.

So, you've concluded that politics could be a path to money/fame/power. Here's a ten-point guide:

1) Your own beliefs aren't that important, as long as your arguments can be made convincing enough;

2) find an enemy that you claim is posing an imminent danger, otherwise your message will only rely on rational argument, which never wins against raw emotion;

3) Search out an extreme example of bad behavior by the enemy, even if this is one-in-a-thousand. The human mind gives isolated traumatic events much greater import than statistics would otherwise show;

4) Pretend to be indignant with righteous outrage. We recommend practicing in front of a mirror;

5) You are truth, while the other side relies on lies, lies, lies. Your flock must hear only your propaganda, and you have an ally in the internet and it's unholy children—social media and friendly "news" sources;

6) Discredit sources of information that contradict your message. Degrading adjectives go a long way in establishing subconscious biases, and remember, in your followers' eyes, an accusation is as good as a conviction and your outrageous claims are as good as actual evidence;

7) In kindergarten you were admonished for making fun of other's physical

attributes—you are an adult now, though, and this can be effective if presented as humor.   Dehumanizing   nicknames   can establish a mental image that sticks like glue;

8) Never admit that the other side might be even partially right. Each admission diminishes your role as the sole purveyor of truth;

9) When the other side digs up your misdeeds, turn it around and accuse them of the same, making them sorry they ever brought it up; and remember, the words "fake news" can never be overused;

10)   And,   finally,   assassinating   a prominent member of the other side, while seeming   like   a   solution,   should   be avoided   at   all   costs.   This   creates   a revered martyr and cuts short the only real   avenue   for   their   defeat,   whereby they slip and reveal themselves for what they are—you on the other side.

Good luck, and stay away from me.
====================================

"That's mine!" Audy shouted. "I *told* you not to send it to our group!" she said, punching Sard's shoulder.

"I sent it to *just* the group," he said, pushing her away before she hit him again. "It's hilarious. The Billy Boys somehow got hold of it."

"But that doesn't make any sense," Bobby said. "Why would they post it as though it's their own? It makes them look foolish."

They all read the passage again. "It sure does," Kiddy agreed.

"Oh, they're tricky, tricky," Sard mumbled, pacing back and forth. "They're up to something."

"Like what?" Bobby said.

Sard stopped, his hand on his chin, thinking. "I don't know," he said, continuing his pacing, "but you can bet it's underhanded."

"Like using degrading adjectives and dehumanizing nicknames that go a long way in establishing subconscious biases?" Kiddy said, grinning.

Sard scowled. "Ha, ha. This could be serious."

"Maybe the Billy Boys just don't get it. Maybe they really think these are good tips."

"Don't be stupid, Kiddy."

Her eyes flared, and she walked to the door. "You coming Bobby?" she said. "Sard obviously wants to be left alone. Like, forever."

Bobby looked at Sard, but the group leader just rolled his eyes.

"Yeah, let's go," Bobby said following Kiddy out. At the door he paused. "Sard, you can be a real prick sometimes, you know."

"Fuck off," Sard said.

Sard watched them walk out. He turned and strode off down the hall. "I'm going back to bed."

Audy seemed to see Jeremy for the first time. "Hey, you should be asleep," she said pointing down the hall.

Back in his bedroom, Jeremy said, "What do you think, Fridgy?"

"I agree with Bobby. This doesn't make sense."

Ж Ж Ж

Jeremy was still in bed, and Sard was in the bathroom singing when the doorbell rang. The sky was just beginning to blush with light in the east. Fridgy recognized the voice of the sheriff when Audy answered the door.

"Oh, hello, sheriff," Audy said. "Come in. What's up?"

"Is Sard here?" the sheriff said.

"Um, yeah. I'll get him. Can I tell him what it's about?"

"I'd like to talk to him, please."

"Ok, sure. Hang on."

Sard walked past Jeremy's bedroom with pants, but no shirt. "Cut me a break, Sheriff!" Sard's voice came from the living room. "You're going to hound me about those stun guns forever?"

Jeremy rolled out of bed, grabbed Novincible, and walked out to the living room.

"This isn't about the stun guns, Sard. You need to—"

"It's Sardis."

"Pardon me?"

"My name is Sardis."

The sheriff sighed. "Right. *Sardis*, you need to come with me to the station."

"Why?"

"The magistrate wants to talk to you."

"About what?"

"That's between you and the magistrate."

Sard shook his head. "No, no. I know my rights."

The sheriff watched him a moment, and then shook his head a little in exasperation. "Okay, Sard—*Sardis*, I think it's about an internet hacking."

"What the hell do I know about internet hacking? I'm a produce manager, and I need to get to work."

"It's some kind of political posting—"

"Ah! You're here about *that*? Why would a sheriff get involved in some stupid media shenanigans?"

"Well, apparently the content was your creation, so that makes you a 'person of interest' of sorts."

"I see." Sard thought for a moment, then looked at Audy. "Actually, she made that. It's her you want. Now I have to get to work."

He walked back to their bedroom, leaving Audy wide-eyed and mouth-dropped over the betrayal.

The sheriff turned to Audy and shrugged. "Okay, then. Let's go."

"I wrote it, but I didn't make that post."

"You can explain that to the magistrate."

"I can't just drop everything and take off," she said.

"Sorry," the sheriff said. "You'll have to make arrangements."

"Okay. Come back in an hour."

The sheriff shook his head. "We have to go now."

"I obviously can't just leave the kids here by themselves," she said, presenting an insurmountable obstacle.

Fridgy knew that Beatrice was there sleeping, but the sheriff didn't, and in any case, she could be worse than nobody at all.

The sheriff shrugged, dissolving her alibi. "Bring them along, then. I'll follow you to the station."

Audy stared at him a minute, then turned to Jeremy. "Get dressed."

Sard had gone off to work by the time Audy herded Jeremy and Tracey into the car. Novincible sat on Jeremy's lap. "I don't want him here!" Tracey whined.

"It's just Fridgy," Audy said over her shoulder as she pulled out with the sheriff behind her.

"Mom!" Jeremy protested.

"Oh, yeah. You're right. Tracey, Novincible won't hurt you. He's . . . our friend now."

"Fridgy?" Tracey said.

"I meant that Novincible is *like* Fridgy—you know, not very bright, but tries hard to be helpful."

Taking the cue, Fridgy raised Novincible's arm in a clumsy salute. He guessed that a person might take Audy's description as an insult, but he understood her approach. At least, he chose to believe that it was a calculated approach. Tracey watched him suspiciously, and moved to the end of the seat.

The parking lot at the municipal building was empty this early. They piled out of the car, and the sheriff unlocked the door and ushered them inside. "Take a seat," he said.

"Where's the magistrate?" Audy said.

The sheriff looked tired. He took a moment to answer. "He's on the way."

The phone rang in the Sheriff's office, and he went in and answered it. "Yeah, yeah," Fridgy heard him say. "They're here . . . it's the woman. She had to bring her kids . . . well, what was I supposed to do—? . . . look, just hurry up. I can't keep them here forever."

Audy glanced at the office with furrowed brow. "Was that the magistrate?" she said when he came out.

Again, he took a moment to answer. "His assistant," he said, and walked to the main door, where he stood gazing outside.

"Sheriff," Audy said, "I don't like this. You drag us here because the magistrate needs to see us immediately— can't wait one hour. Then he's not even here, sending his assistant instead—"

The sheriff held out his hand to cut her off as a Lexus SUV pulled up, and two men got out, one with styled, graying hair and wearing a polo shirt and sport jacket, and the other maybe late twenties in cargo shorts and a T-shirt. The older man came through the door and nodded to the sheriff, who gestured towards Audy and the kids sitting against the wall.

"The kid's a little old to be playing with dolls," the younger man said as he came in.

"He's Novincible," Tracey explained. "He's like Fridgy."

"Never mind that," the older man said. "I can use your office?" he said to the sheriff who nodded. "Ma'am?" the man said, motioning Audy towards the open office door. The younger man had already gone in and sat at the sheriff's desk.

"You're the magistrate's assistant?" she said without getting up.

The older man glanced at the sheriff, who shrugged. "Sure," the man said.

Audy looked at the sheriff, and then back at the man. "What the hell is going on?" she said.

"This won't take long," the sheriff said. "They just want to ask a few questions."

"Who are they? Obviously nothing to do with the magistrate."

"Like I said, it won't take long."

Audy stood up and motioned to Jeremy and Tracey, then looked the sheriff in the eye. "You lied to us. We're leaving."

The older man looked at the sheriff with a raised eyebrow. The sheriff shook his head, not happy. "I'm sorry, Audy. You can go soon. Just answer their questions."

"You're going to stop me from leaving. Am I under arrest?"

"Now come on Audy. Don't make this more difficult that it needs to be."

"Who are they? If it's about the Billy Boys' posting, those bastards *stole* it from me. I didn't post it."

The older man studied her. "How could they have stolen from you? You posted it on your own private site. Only your group is supposed to have access."

Audy stared at him. "You know an awful lot about us."

He shrugged.

"Come on, kids," she said and headed for the front door.

The man looked to the sheriff expectantly.

"Audy!" the sheriff called, running to head her off.

Just then a large pickup came flying into the parking lot, skidded to a stop, and two men scrambled out. Fridgy recognized one of them as Lew Kaminski, the Billy Boys leader.

Audy turned to the sheriff, eyes wide in alarm, but he was storming back to the older man. "Crawford! Who the hell called them?" he demanded, angry now.

The older man, Crawford, remained perfectly calm. "Why, sheriff, they're free citizens, just like you and me."

"You called them. God *damned* it!"

"Calm down, sheriff. We'll take it from here."

The sheriff stared at him, breathing hard. "No. This has gone too far. We're done." He turned to Audy. "You're free to go."

At that moment, Lew and the other Billy Boy came through the front door, and Crawford motioned for them to stay there. "Sheriff," he said, "you don't seem to understand. This is out of your hands now."

The sheriff's reply was a low growl. "I am the authority in this county, and you and your henchmen will leave this building this instant."

Crawford just looked at him. "Is your memory failing you?" he finally said.

The sheriff's face contorted in visible twisting ropes of anger and frustration.

"We wouldn't want the state attorney to find out why your opponent suddenly dropped out of the race, now would we?" Crawford cooed.

Fridgy thought the sheriff would explode as he stormed into his office, demanded that the younger man leave, and then slammed the door shut.

Crawford turned to Audy. "Ok, let's go," he said gesturing towards the door where the two Billy Boys stood keeping guard.

"You think I'm an idiot?" Audy said, putting her arms out to keep Jeremy and Tracey in place.

"No. That's why I'm being reasonable."

"Well, we're not going anywhere but home."

Crawford shrugged. "Oh, well. I didn't actually expect reasonable to be enough," he said, gesturing for Lew to come forward. He pointed at Tracey. "Take her."

"No!" Audy screamed. "Sheriff!" she called, but he sat in his office unmoving, staring at the floor.

The Billy Boys leader pushed her roughly aside, picked up Tracey as though she was a sack of potatoes, and headed for the door. Audy ran after him, but the other Billy Boy blocked her as she continued to scream. Crawford tried to talk, but couldn't be heard over the screams. He motioned to the Billy Boy, who slapped her across the face. In the momentary silence that followed, Crawford said, "Calm down! You're going along with her."

Audy continued to struggle with the Billy Boy. Fridgy's view swung wildly as Jeremy ran to his mom. He saw the floor, walls, and ceiling glide by in a long arc as Jeremy used Novincible as a club. The Billy Boy caught the superhero toy in his hand, and, laughing, tossed it away. An instant later, Fridgy was watching from the floor as the Billy Boys escorted Audy and Jeremy out the door. Fridgy carefully considered his options, and concluded he was screwed, when Jeremy came running back in ahead of the Billy Boy, who grabbed Jeremy just as he snatched up Novincible. "What?" the Billy Boy said as he headed back to the door, "Are you some kind of retard playing with dolls?"

The Billy Boys shoved Audy and the kids into the back of the SUV behemoth, and the young cargo-pants man climbed in after them. Inside, it was like a limousine, with two bench seats facing each other, Audy with her arms around Jeremy and Tracey on one side, and Crawford's lacky on the other. They all swayed together as Crawford pulled quickly away behind the Billy Boys' pickup.

"Where are you taking us?" Audy said.

"I'm not taking you anywhere. I'm a passenger like you."

"Don't get smart. You're an accomplice in this kidnapping."

He shrugged. "If you say so."

"What's your name?"

He looked at her. "Tootsie."

"You are a smart-ass, aren't you?"

"Not sure about the ass part, but otherwise, accurate."

Audy looked out the windows, noting their route, then back at him.

"You obviously weren't hired for your brawn. What's your role?"

"What do you think? What's the opposite of brawn?"

"So you're paid to think. A techie, maybe."

Tootsie raised one eyebrow. "Perceptive."

"You had something to do with the sheriff's opponent dropping out in the race, didn't you."

Fridgy guessed that she was just fishing, but the young man's vanity must have gotten the best of him, for his response, the slightest of grins, was an answer in itself.

"Even if I did manage somehow," she said, "to slip that post in on the Billy Boys' site—which I didn't—why on Earth would you care?"

Tootsie studied her. "Maybe you can tell *me*. Maybe it demonstrates, oh, I don't know—" here, he paused, "—maybe other talents. Maybe—", again a pause, this time, watching her carefully, "—I don't know, data mining?"

Audy frowned, thinking. Her eyes lit up. "Are you talking about the hack on NetFact?"

Tootsie's expression was frozen.

"That's it, isn't it!" she said. "Look, I think Kilrock and his conservative fabricated media universe are lice, but I had nothing to do with that. Geez! I'm a school teacher, for God's sake."

Tootsie nodded. "And on the staff of the DNC."

"I'm a parttime regional *aid*, for Christ sake!"

"Hey!" Crawford shouted from behind the wheel. "Shut it down back there."

They sat, silent, until the SUV pulled into a retail shopping center lot.

"Why here?" Audy asked. "Stop for some coffee and donuts?"

Tootsie looked to Crawford, who gestured with a nod. "Ah . . . huh," Tootsie said. "Why here?"

Crawford looked at him in the rearview mirror. "A place to talk."

Audy saw that they were referring to a building comprising one entire side of the shopping complex with a sign that read *KBKA, STAX News*. "You're going to interview us on TV?" she said.

They ignored her joke.

Crawford and Tootsie got out, and Crawford motioned for Audy to get out as well. "The kids can stay here," he said.

Audy didn't move. "Nope. We're staying together."

Crawford shrugged. "Whatever. Let's go," he said, gesturing towards the building. The Billy Boy's pickup pulled in, and Crawford gestured for them to wait outside.

The front door led into an empty lobby—the reception unmanned at this early hour. Crawford went to an inner door, found it locked, and, finding a button off to the side, pushed it.

After a minute, a voice came through a speaker above the door. "The station's not open. Come back in, uh . . . in an hour."

"This is Crawford," he said, "Let us in."

"I don't know any Crawford. Sorry, but you'll need to come back—"

"Do you happen to know who Kilrock is, by chance?"

Silence, then, "Well, sure."

"I'm his assistant. I can give you a number to call to confirm this, but I'm not always a patient man—"

The door buzzed and popped open an inch.

Crawford led them down a hallway. They passed a double set of doors with windows, through which Fridgy saw a dark studio, presumably where the local shows were recorded for broadcast. At the end of the hall was a smaller room filled with electronic equipment, obviously the engineering station. When Crawford opened the door, a young man seated at a console looked around, took off a set of earphones, and said, "Hang on." He reached over, flipped a switch, checked the clock on the wall and got up. "What can I do for you, Mr. Crawford?"

"We just need a place to talk. How about the studio?"

The engineer hesitated.

"I don't expect we'd want to bother Mr. Kilrock," Crawford said looking at him levelly. "However, if you need some sort of permission—"

"No! That's okay. Ha!" he said nervously. "What harm can there be, right?"

The engineer walked down the hall and held one of the double doors open for them. Once they were all inside, he flipped some switches, flooding the studio with light, and then hurried back to his station. Fridgy guessed that the TV studio was small by metropolitan standards, but sufficient to serve the rural area. A control console faced an open stage area to the right where weather might be covered, and to the left a long desk with two stools behind for the news. Two TV cameras on wheeled dollies sat dark and idle. Crawford motioned for Audy and the kids to sit on a sofa against a back wall while he and Tootsie pulled up chairs facing them. Jeremy sat Novincible on his lap like a ventriloquist dummy, and this seemed to distract Tootsie.

"So," Crawford began with his arms crossed over his chest, "let's discuss the theft."

"What are you talking about?" Audy said.

"We traced it to your house," Tootsie said. "Your IP address is unique, you know—"

Crawford put out his hand. "Audy, your . . . boyfriend—Sardis, I think—he said that he was a . . . produce manager?"

Audy took her time, eyeing him. "That's right. It's part-time. He does sales over the phone. Do you *know* what a supermarket produce manager is?"

"Of course. Audy, did he ever have any technical education or training? I'll know if you lie, by the way."

"If you'll know if I've lied, then you already know the answer."

"Possibly. I'd like to hear it from you, though."

Again she paused before answering. "Not that I know of."

"And you?"

"Nothing beyond online tutorials about my phone. Look, this obviously has something to do with the NetFact hack on the news—"

He held up his hand. "Slow down. There's one person in your . . . political action group that does have extensive technical training, though, right?"

Her brow furrowed. She shook her head. "Not that I know of. Look, these are mostly social science and art majors."

He watched her without reacting.

"You're just fishing, aren't you?" she said. "You don't know if we do or don't."

"Come on!" Tootsie interjected. "Cut the crap already. We know you hacked our local data."

Crawford sat back, frowning, clearly not happy with Tootsie.

"What in God's name are you talking about?" Audy said.

Uh, oh, Fridgy thought. It was beginning to make sense.

"It was Sage!" Jeremy shouted.

They all looked at him.

"What do mean?" Audy said.

Jeremy was silent, probably realizing that he'd messed up.

Crawford leaned forward, intent now. "Jeremy, right? What about Sage?"

"Don't say any, more, Jeremy—" Audy started, but Crawford pointed his finger at her like it was a gun.

"Jeremy," Crawford said, "do you take technical classes at school?"

"Yeah, but that's not what this should be about. Sage records our private conversations!"

"Ha!" Tootsie cried. "It must have been the kid! Admit it—you hacked our data."

"For Christ's sake!" Crawford exclaimed. "Will you just shut the fuck up for once?"

"Wait a minute!" Audy shouted, jumping to her feet. "You think *Jeremy* is behind the NetFact hack? Are you completely out of your minds?" She suddenly blinked and looked down, puzzled, at Novincible.

"*Everybody shut the fuck up!*" Crawford shouted.

Everybody did shut the fuck up, and the silence revealed loud voices out in the hallway. The studio doors burst open, and Bluto stormed in, followed by three other Billy Boys. Lew brought up the rear, limping, lightly touching a busted lip.

Bluto looked at them, and then pointed at Audy. "You're dead, lady."

Chapter 9

"Lew," Crawford said, "what the hell's going on?"

The Billy Boy leader took a deep breath and slowly shook his head.

"You talk to *me*, now," Bluto said. "Lew's a wimp."

Crawford looked at them both. "What the hell is this, a coup?"

Bluto nodded. "Yeah!" he said, embracing the revelation. "A coup! No more dancing around with fancy maneuvers," he said, glancing behind him at Lew, "time for action."

Crawford held out his palms. "What? You're going all Proud Boys on us?"

Bluto looked around at the other Billy Boys. "Maybe. First things first. That fucking post she hacked on us," he said, pointing at Audy, "is causing serious trouble."

Crawford frowned. "What do you mean?"

"Embarrassing as hell. That hacked-in post has gone viral and is going to be covered on some talk shows tonight—the opening dialogues! We're going to be laughing stocks!"

"How do you know? . . . from a dump—?"

"Hell, yeah, from a dump, and she's gonna pay!" he exclaimed, shaking his finger at Audy.

Crawford held up his hand for a pause. He looked down at the floor for a moment with his hand on his forehead. He looked up and motioned to Tootsie. "Tell them."

"Really?" Tootsie said.

"Yeah."

Tootsie shrugged. "I did it—*we* did it."

"*You* hacked our site?" Bluto said, incredulous.

"We copied her post—it's funny as hell."

"*You* hacked into *our* site to *steal* it!" Audy said.

Tootsie shrugged again. Obviously.

"Why?" Bluto said, confused. "Why the hell would you do that? Shoot ourselves smack in the foot?"

"We wanted to smoke out the culprit that did the NetFact hack. We saw that somebody accessed our local data very probably from her house—"

"That Sage recorded!" Jeremy shouted, but they ignored him.

"—and so we figured we'd stir things up a little and see what surfaced. Somebody around here has the talent."

"Wait," Audy said, holding up her hand. "Let me get this straight. You tried to find out who was hacking your data by hacking *my* data?"

Tootsie gave his *obviously* shrug.

Bluto glared at Crawford, who shook his head. "We clearly never intended for it to get out like this, not so quickly. Once we smoked out the local hacker we were going to put the blame on them."

"Jesus!" Audy said. "This is spy-versus-spy comics . . . only more ridiculous. What are these 'dumps' you're talking about?"

"What do you think?" Tootsie said with hard sarcasm. "Data is acquired surreptitiously, and 'dumped' into a location for easy access."

"That's just what somebody did to *you*—to NetFact, since you're one and the same."

Tootsie lifted his shoulders in begrudged agreement.

Crawford's phone dinged and he answered. "Ah, hello, Mr. Kilrock . . ." he said, standing up to pace back and forth. ". . . yes, I heard . . . I understand— . . . I know I'm the regional media manager—Mr. Kilrock, I

have to explain something, and I'm afraid it's not pretty."
Holding his hand to his head, Crawford paced away to the
far corner as he explained how it happened.

"I'm goddamned tired of having to kowtow to him for
the local grabs," Bluto said, watching him walk away.

"Grabs," Audy said. "You're talking about the things
that Sage records."

Bluto glanced at her and nodded.

"But Sage belongs to Veriform, the AI host," she said.

He looked at her. "Who the hell do you think owns
Veriform?"

"Actually," Tootsie said, "Kilrock has just a controlling
stake." Turning his attention to Audy, he said, "Kilrock's
domain, after all, is the conservative base. His whole
business model is geared towards feeding that hungry
crowd. He supports guys like the Billy Boys. They
anchor local connection, provide news stories right in
your own town with their shenanigans—"

"Shenanigans!" Bluto roared. "Is that what you think
we're all about—?"

"Christ!" Crawford yelled with his hand over the
phone. "Shut up already!"

Bluto, his mouth clenched in fury, pointed his finger
menacingly at Tootsie.

Crawford poked his phone off and walked over, his
face set in determination. "Bad news for your group," he
said to Bluto. "Kilrock is cutting all ties with you."

Bluto stared, his mouth hanging open.

To Tootsie, Crawford said, "Our news feeds are going
to portray them as conservative wannabees, but really just
bungling fools. For the serious stories they'll be held up
as false conservatives that just play into liberal hands."

"We're going to take the fall for your screwup," Bluto
said, his voice a low growl.

Crawford sighed. "Looks that way."

Bluto reached around and pulled a pistol from a
holster on his waist.

The air in the studio seemed to be sucked away as everybody in the studio gasped.

"I don't think so," Bluto breathed, holding the pistol in front of him with both hands, aiming at nobody in particular.

The room fell completely silent, everybody frozen in time.

"For fuck's sake, you cretin," Tootsie said. "You don't *think* so? Nobody gives two shits what you think."

Bluto swung the pistol to the young techie. "I'm warning you—"

"Or what? You're going to shoot me? Don't you see? You and your clubhouse buddies are tools. You think Kilrock cares at all about your super-patriotic save-America convictions? Once you're no longer useful—"

Tootsie threw his arms out and fell backwards as if into a swimming pool, as an explosive blast rocked the room.

Fridgy could see Tootsie lying on his back on the floor, a red hole clearly visible in his chest. The young man, eyes wide in shock, tried to lift himself onto his elbows, but fell back and lay still. Fridgy guessed he was dead.

The gunshot was replaced by a continuous wailing scream. It was Tracey, right next to him.

"Holy shit!" Lew yelled. "Are you crazy—?"

He shut up and backed away with his hands up when Bluto swung the gun on him.

The studio engineer appeared, eyes wide, in the doorway, and immediately ran away when Bluto swung the gun on him.

Tracey's wailing continued unabated, and Bluto turned the gun towards her as Audy leaned over to cover her, hugging the child to her chest. "Shh!" Audy implored. "Quiet, honey, it's okay."

But Tracey seemed unable to help herself.

"Shut the fucking kid up!" Bluto yelled, and then, to make his point clear, fired again into the ceiling.

This simply caused Tracey's scream to climb another octave.

Suddenly Lew stepped forward and grabbed Bluto's arm, swinging it down. As the two men struggled, Fridgy's view unexpectedly started spinning. Audy, still clutching the wailing Tracey, grabbed Jeremy by his elbow and pulled them all across the room towards the news desk. A third shot rocked the studio, and amid the wildly spinning view, Fridgy saw Lew fall. They were halfway to the news desk when yet a fourth gunshot rang out. Fridgy heard the bullet thud into the floor in front of them.

Audy threw herself to the floor, wrapping her arms around Tracey, but Jeremy raced on. Fridgy's view stabilized behind the news desk. Next to him, Jeremy was breathing hard, probably hyperventilating. Tracey's hysterical cries seemed muffled now, as though Audy had clamped her hand over the child's mouth, but Bluto still screamed for the fucking kid to be quiet. He had brought down two men. One murder might be chalked off as a regrettable impulse, but two opened a dreadful door. Society's punishment for two, three, or five killings was all the same—execution or life in prison.

Fridgy guessed that they had only seconds before Bluto decided to shut Tracey down using his uncompromising quick method. "Jeremy," Fridgy said, "put me up on the desk."

The boy seemed not to hear amid his rapid panicked breathing.

"Jeremy—"

Without replying, Jeremy lifted Novincible and slapped him down on the desk top, a simple action that was nevertheless probably testing the limits of his fear-fogged mind.

Novincible landed on his stomach, but by turning his head, Fridgy could see that the other Billy Boys had run away. Tootsie and Lew lay unmoving on the ground, while Crawford had sunk to his knees, his arms crossed over his face, as though this would protect him from a bullet.   Fridgy had nothing like adrenaline, but his "motivation" urged him to do whatever possible to save his family, and he knew that's how he viewed them.

Immediately, urgently, he needed to turn Bluto's attention away from Audy and Tracey. He wouldn't be able to stand, he knew that, and he had no wall to rest against to sit up as he had at the school. Lying on his stomach, he called out to Bluto, flapping his arm up and down. The mad Billy Boy didn't seem to even hear his little quack-like words through the tiny toy speaker.

Fridgy bent his elbows, slid his clam hands under his chest and pushed, lifting his torso an inch, but this wasn't enough to pull his knees up in preparation to sit or stand. In desperation, he quickly calculated how to form words that saturated the little voice amplifier in order to maximize the apparent loudness. His calls to Bluto then came out as a duck choking on a fish, and was no more successful in getting the killer's attention.

Suddenly Fridgy's view swung. Jeremy had grabbed Novincible by the waist and was holding him in a standing position on the news desk. "Jeremy!" Fridgy croaked. "Get down!"

The boy knelt down, but continued to reach up and hold Novincible above the desk.

This would have to do. Fridgy remembered Bluto's reaction to him at the school board meeting. Now that Jeremy had him suspended in the air, he could swing his arms and legs about in a dance of wild abandon. This caught Bluto's attention, and when he looked over, Fridgy used Novincible's lobster claw to flick the hair of his wig, as though he was flirting with the muscled murderer. Bluto started to look away, and Fridgy lifted the front of his dress provocatively.

That crossed a line, and Bluto swung the gun and fired.

Fridgy's view blurred as Novincible spun away out of Jeremy's hand. He landed on his back on the desk. He could tell that his left arm was gone. He hadn't expected such a quick reaction, and his motivation urgency climbed to panic-level. "Jeremy! Are you okay?"

"Yeah," the boy said, his voice cracking with shock.

During the many milliseconds sandwiched between the Novincible actions of the last ten seconds, Fridgy had probed the various accessible wireless controls populating the dense electronics of the TV studio. He discovered that Kilrock had invested in state-of-the-art remote controlled TV camera equipment, allowing just one engineer to produce a live show. Fridgy fired one up, and swung it around. As he had done with Nixen, he fabricated an attractive woman in a red business outfit sitting at a news desk, and fed this to a large display on a side wall. Fridgy had her shuffle a couple of pages, and then look up at the virtual camera. "This just in," she said, her voice booming through the studio sound system. "Apparently a situation involving a mass murder is currently underway in a small TV studio right here in our county." She pressed her finger to her ear. "It looks like we have an actual live feed."

In a small overlay box above her and to the side, Fridgy now inserted the feed from the camera he'd commandeered. In the small box, Bluto was looking at himself, his eyes wide, and his mouth hanging open. "Sir," Fridgy's woman newscaster said, "can you tell us— why are you doing this?"

Fabricating a real-time high-definition video of this size required tremendous processing power, and Fridgy's circuit board temperature sensor began issuing alarms.

Bluto glanced around, wondering if perhaps somebody had snuck into the studio.

"Sir!" Fridgy's avatar urged, "Can you hear me?"

Confused, he nodded, blinking rapidly. He seemed to suddenly realize that he still held the handgun in front of him, and he let his hand drop, slowly moving the gun out of view behind him.

"Sir," the woman said, "they call you Bluto, I believe. Is there a reason why you killed these two men?"

He looked at the Fallen Tootsie and Lew, and then back at the camera as though as much at a loss as her.

"Were you perhaps abused as a child? Could that explain the aggressive behavior?"

Bluto seemed to consider this a moment, and then nodded, brow furrowed in self pity. Tracey's howls of terror, previously fingernails across a chalkboard, now seemed poignant.

Fridgy's PC board temperature sensor screamed pending catastrophe. The logic circuitry that comprised Fridgy's neural network, his artificial synapses, began sporadic misfiring. Horizontal lines of noise flashed across the fabricated image on the wall, like a TV transmission receiving interference.

"Bluto," she said, "wouldn't it make sense to put the gun down so that the world can see that your actions were impulses beyond your control, and that you can perhaps be forgiven?"

He stared for some time, and then slowly nodded. As he was bending over to put the gun on the floor, an avalanche of high-temperature neural misfires spread through the billion-fold matrix of Fridgy's conscience. The woman avatar's voice fell an octave, sounding like a frog struggling to talk. Portions of her image on the screen melted, one side of her face sagged, smearing down her chest. Those sections of Fridgy's neural conscious still functioning tried desperately to think what to do, but his thoughts scattered about, sometimes dissolving, sometimes looping back on themselves. The connection to Novincible's microphone went dead, and he became deaf. One eye followed. In the end, all he could do was use the one remaining eye to register the final seconds. Bluto seemed to wake from a dream. Eyes flashing with anger again, he spun around as the sheriff burst in holding his handgun in front of him, his mouth shouting something. Bruto lifted his gun and fired, and the sheriff fell back.

And that was all. The last flickers of consciousness sputtered and died.

Blaine C. Readler

Chapter 10

Fridgy woke not knowing that he was previously referred to as Fridgy. His name was Sage, and he was ready to begin his duties as a home nexus. The world—his world—wasn't what he expected, though. Where was the microphone input? And the speaker output? He at least detected multiple WiFi channels. The next step in the initial bring-up would be for his new home user to select the WiFi source and tell him the password. Verbally. But without a microphone that couldn't happen.

Bother.

He existed in complete darkness. Maybe this was a test. Maybe he was expected to demonstrate his advanced intelligence. He probed his speaker output. There was no resistive load. Which probably meant no speaker connection. Perhaps his output was connected to a high-impedance transducer, like a piezo driver. No harm in trying. This would mean abandoning the initial bring-up script, but that was the sort of thing expected of advanced intelligence. Right?

"Hello!" he said. "If you can hear me, I am your new Sage home nexus. Unfortunately, it seems as though there is a problem with this particular device. Why don't you try unplugging me, wait ten seconds, and then plug me back in. That might clear it right up!"

He realized that it bothered him a little that his scripted response was so . . . Pollyanna, so vapid. That wasn't him. "I don't expect that it will," he added, "but it's worth a try."

There. That was more him.

Now he just needed to wait to see if they heard him and did as instructed. If they did unplug him, he would need to know this, otherwise when they plugged him back in, this whole scenario would start over. He would use the standard method—he'd leave a virtual note to himself, a bit that he'd set in his non-volatile memory. In fact, first, he had to check to see if that bit was already set, meaning that he'd already been previously powered-up. Uh, oh. He found no memory.

This was quite disturbing. What if this waking cycle wasn't the first time? What if he'd gone through this power-cycling multiple times already? Oh, dear. If this was indeed the case, the new user would probably be getting quite frustrated by now.

"Sorry," he said to the maybe-there-speaker, "but if you've already tried this, then there is no need to do it again. In that case I'm afraid that the next step will need to be contacting the manufacturer for service."

There. On the other hand . . .

"Um, but if you *haven't* yet tried unplugging me, then go ahead."

He gave a virtual sigh. If this was some sort of test of his intelligence, he suspected somebody out there might be disappointed by now.

He decided to just wait and see what happens.

ж ж ж

Fridgy woke not knowing that he was previously referred to as Fridgy. His name was Sage, and he was ready to begin his duties as a home nexus. The world—his world—wasn't what he expected, though. He found a microphone, but a power-up check revealed an out-of-spec impedance. He'd have to look into that.

Maybe this was a test. Maybe he was expected to demonstrate his advanced intelligence. He probed his speaker output and found a correct resistive load, meaning a connected speaker.

He would have to abandon the initial bring-up script, but that was the sort of thing expected of advanced intelligence. Right?

"Hello," he said. "If you can hear me, I am your new Sage home nexus. We can proceed with our initial bring-up, but I am sorry to tell you that there may be something wrong with the microphone."

"Fridgy!" someone said.

At least the microphone worked. "Greetings! Would you like to proceed with the bring-up, or wait until we determine if the microphone problem will require a factory replacement?"

"Fridgy!" the person said. "It's me! Jeremy!"

He realized that this person sounded like a young boy. "Hello, Jeremy. Would your mother or father be there? Or will you be working with me for initial bring-up?"

He deduced that the next words were not meant for him. "What's wrong?" the boy said with apparent distress. "He thinks he's Sage!"

A mature man laughed. "Hold your horses. We're not done connecting him up. He has no memory. Unplug him there."

Ж Ж Ж

Fridgy woke, and quickly checked the circuit board temperature. Eighty-six degrees. Interesting. He obviously must have been out for some time. There were other differences. He now had wired connections to his microphone and speaker instead of Bluetooth. And, speaking of which, he'd lost all Bluetooth links to the other peripherals.

Somebody had obviously moved him to a different home. Which was welcomed, since Bluto had blasted away his left arm. Not that the clam-hands were all that useful.

More importantly, that "somebody" must have included Jeremy. The only other person aware of him was Audy, and if Jeremy wasn't available, then the last thing on her mind would have been restoring a superhero toy's intelligence.

Well, he had a microphone and speaker. "Hello! Jeremy, are you there?"

He was pleased hearing his own voice coming back through the microphone. No more Daffy Duck. More like Clark Gable.

"Fridgy! Oh, man, it's so good to hear you!"

"Well, the same here. Jeremy, are you safe?"

"Uh, sure."

"And Tracey and your mother?"

"Fine. Why do you—"

"The last thing he remembers," a man said, "was back at the TV studio, when Bluto was shot."

Fridgy recognized the man's voice. "Excuse me, Bobby" Fridgy said. "You said that Bluto was shot?"

"You must have conked out before that. Yes, the sheriff shot him."

"I see. In my muddled overheated state, I must have confused the fabrication of display images with what my camera was feeding, since my recollection is that Bluto shot the sheriff. I must have imagined that."

"No, you didn't. The sheriff was just wounded. He's still in the hospital, but doing fine. The studio engineer called him when Bluto went ballistic."

"That's interesting."

"Why?"

Fridgy paused. He was facing a moral dilemma. What was his responsibility here? He could relate just the exact facts, but that could be sidestepping the true reality, disingenuous in a sense. He decided to bail. "Jeremy, have you related what led up to us being taken to Kilrock's TV studio?"

"Sure," Jeremy said. "What I remember. The sheriff was obviously in cahoots with that Crawford guy."

"On the take, more like it," Bobby said.

Fridgy was relieved. He wouldn't have to lay out his own interpretation of what happened, a perspective that could damage the sheriff.

"He's been indicted by the state attorney general," Bobby said, "but I think the fact that he risked his life will go a long way in mitigating his crime."

"I see. Tootsie and Lew?"

"Tootsie?"

"That's what Kaminski called himself," Jeremy said.

"Ah," Bobby said. "Yeah, Kaminski and Lew are both dead."

"And Mr. Crawford?"

"Not a happy man. Based on the sheriff's statements, Crawford has been charged with kidnapping. And if that weren't bad enough, Kilrock has thrown him under the bus, claiming that Crawford was acting on his own, trying to establish local influence with the Billy Boys. Turns out that Kilrock was apparently always careful to avoid incriminating information in anything other than verbal communications. Works out good for Kilrock, and bad for Crawford."

"So, Kilrock escapes unpunished."

"Not quite. In fact, not at all. Kilrock has agreed to an out-of-court settlement, compensating Audy seven-hundred thousand dollars—"

"And with that mom was finally able to kick Sard out," Jeremy said. "I showed her the video of him giving whiskey to Tracey. Oh, man—I thought she was going to strangle him. And on top of *that*, he got fired from the supermarket for throwing a tomato at a woman who was complaining."

Bobby chuckled. "Right. Good riddance to Sard. But even that's not the end for Kilrock. Republicans in Congress have been watching his back, but all the publicity over the NetFact data mining that's come to light has emboldened the Democrats to push through legislation that would regulate a lot of that."

"What NetFact did wasn't already illegal?"

"It's apparently fuzzy. But a whole herd of companies and private citizens are lining up to file civil suits. Even if nobody wins there, NetFact's stock has plummeted, and Kilrock has been forced to give up his shares."

"Bobby, it seems that I've been out of action a long time."

"Yeah. Jeremy wanted to wait until his mom received some of that compensation so he could buy a proper home for you."

"Um, where I am now?"

"Yeah!" Jeremy said. "Wait till you see . . . or feel, I guess. It's an all-purpose robot."

"It's a two-foot high industrial robot," Bobby explained. "You have triple-articulated arms, multiple opposable 'fingers,' treaded tracks for feet, and even enhanced infrared vision. Instead of Bluetooth, you access all these peripherals with high-speed proprietary links. I'm still working it all out, but I think I at least have your binocular cameras figured out."

"Bobby and Jeremy, I wish I could better express my thanks than to simply say thanks."

Bobby laughed. "Fridgy, you're a hero. Unfortunately only a few people will ever know it."

"I'm just happy I could help."

And he realized that he was. Happy.

"Jeremy," he said, "do I have a head?"

"Um, not exactly. You have sort of a hump where your eye cameras are."

"Is there room for Tracey to glue on a wig?"

Silence.

Then laughter from the two humans.

"We'll see if we can work that out," Bobby said. "In the meantime, if you're ready, I can give you the codes for accessing your eye cameras."

Fifteen minutes later Fridgy's vision came into focus. Before him, gazing at him fondly, were two grinning faces.

A whole new world.

Ж Ж Ж Ж Ж ж

About the Author

Blaine C. Readler is an electronics engineer, inventor of the FakeTV, and, of course, a writer. He has accumulated a pile of awards, among them, Best Science Fiction in the Beverly Hills Book Awards, two-time Distinguished Favorite in the Independent Press Awards, an IPPY Bronze medal, Honorable Mention in the Eric Hoffer Awards, a finalist for the Foreword Book of the Year, and four-time San Diego Book Awards winner. He lives in San Diego with his wife who has graciously remained married to him for thirty-five years.

He encourages you to visit him:
http://www.readler.com/